Tales from Down on the Farm

Tales from Down on the Farm

BEDTIME STORIES
FOR ANXIOUS CHILDREN

BY

LESLEY GLOVER

Strategic Book Publishing and Rights Co.

Strategic Book Publishing and Rights Co.
12620 FM 1960, Suite A4-507
Houston, TX 77065
www.sbpra.com

For information about special discounts for bulk purchases, please conttact Strategic Book Publishing and Rights Co. Special Sales, at bookorder@sbpra.net

ISBN: 978-1-62857-055-7

Book Design by Julius Kiskis

21 22 20 19 18 17 16 15 14   1 2 3 4 5

Contents

Preface

I first began to write my stories at the request of friends whose children were having problems with lack of confidence, concentration, and other anxiety issues at school. I felt that using animals to tell a story was the best metaphorical way of getting messages across to help the child progress, and by being in their own comfortable surroundings, they would be able to avoid those awkward and limiting feelings of shyness that usually arise when meeting a stranger.

The stories helped the children, who responded by asking for more.

In order to help them with their anxieties, I felt that the best way was to encourage them to explore their own feelings of low self-esteem and lack of confidence which underlie the many issues that they have today and to work out the answers for themselves.

Animals, by their very nature, learn by observing, mimicking, and experimenting, and so it was by watching my own animals, especially a kitten called Bo, at play, that I began to use the lessons they showed me as a way to write my stories. By using those lessons, I hoped they would encourage the children to understand themselves a little more and make the positive steps in their lives count. By knowing and understanding what life's lessons are all about, we learn from the mistakes we make and have the courage to try something new.

Confidence and self-esteem are how we learn to adapt and modify our behaviour on a daily basis. The animals in the stories show us how to look at life's problems differently in order to find the solution, because when we're successful in rising above the problem, our confidence levels rise and we feel better about ourselves.

By reading these stories at bedtime or during a quiet time in the day, the subtle, yet poignant suggestions encased within the storylines are absorbed by the child's creative and imaginative mind in the comfort and safety of his or her own surroundings; so when he or she falls asleep, the mind continues to process these positive verbal suggestions. Even if the child falls asleep, the story needs to be read to the end, as the mind continues to hear and absorb the spoken words. Hence, there are no pictures in this book to distract from those positive messages.

I wrote the stories to be read aloud by the parents for several reasons; first, it gives the child and parent precious time together which is healing in itself; second, I felt that the thought-provoking suggestions and questions would help the parent to look at his or her own problems and issues from a different angle, thus helping him or her to address his or her own needs. Children are very sensitive and many reflect their parent's anxieties, whilst the parent worries more about their child's fears and worries, instead of attending to his or her own.

I have also incorporated within the stories the need to recognise and understand that mistakes in life happen; we are not perfect and perfection is only an ideal. The reality is we make mistakes and learn from them, but unfortunately, trying to get it right the first time and failing can increase the feelings of anxiety and stress in some.

My stories are about building confidence and self-esteem and exploring emotions and feelings, whilst developing a sense of fun and laughter, so that life can be enjoyed in a less serious way.

Enjoy.

Acknowledgments

I would like to acknowledge my friends, Renee and Zoe, who asked me to write some stories to help their children overcome personal issues. Their continued support and encouragement to write more bedtime stories for children helped me to overcome my own personal hurdle of self-belief.

I would like to thank the many children who read my first stories and encouraged me to continue, by asking for more.

I would also like to thank Sally for her support and encouragement whilst reading my stories long into the night.

Story Guide

"Mr. Bo Jangles" is about understanding limitations and thus avoiding disappointments. It highlights the need to learn as an on-going process of life.

"Misty Blue" is about how being selfish and stubborn and not understanding the need to co-operate or take into consideration the needs of others affects those with whom you share your life.

"The Penny Drops with Misty" brings about the recognition that stubbornness gets you nowhere, and by understanding its negative imprint, then the ability to change it can be employed.

"Oh! How Naughty Can They Be?" suggests that it's good to have fun, laugh, and enjoy doing the little things in life without being too serious about what might happen.

"Annie Meets Plumpkin" is about facing fears and understanding that with the right frame of mind, you can overcome them. It's also about building confidence that increases as the control of fear diminishes.

"The Circus Came to Town" encourages the discovery of new skills and abilities, as working together with a positive state of mind builds confidence.

"It Wasn't Easy" tries to illustrate that by recognising limitations and being honest about them, it gives encouragement to change and alters the focus of intent.

"Eddie, the Wise Owl" offers a lesson in understanding that new things can be learned when a different approach is applied. It also encourages confidence so one can speak out and learn to accept praise with sincerity.

"Monty" is about how being over confident can get you into trouble, but understanding personal limitations can actually assist in making you feel more confident.

"What Dreams Are Made Of" tries to illustrate how our minds work and that because they are programmable, given the right positive information, the capacity for learning new things can be enhanced.

"Bo to the Rescue" is about how thinking one thing can make it real. Happiness is a state of mind that is created by our actions and affects those around us.

"Bo, the Explorer" helps to reinforce confidence and illustrates that it's acceptable to ask for help to solve a problem.

"Annie Meets Sinbad" helps in conquering fears and how understanding failure helps to stimulate positive actions, body language, respect, and confidence.

"When the Moon Turned Orange" is about the changes and cycles that are normal in our everyday lives, so they shouldn't be misunderstood or feared.

"Sleepy Time," when spoken in soft tones, helps soothe the child into a nice, comfortable place that brings about sleep, while reinforcing suggestions for calmness and confidence.

Mr. Bo Jangles

Once upon a sunny, summer's day, a litter of eight kittens were born in a hammock down on the farm, and I was one of them. It was really a bit of old sacking tied at one end to a rusty old tractor and at the other end to a dusty old door post, and I have to say it was quite a tight squeeze until the human moved us, so that we had room to grow and stretch our tiny legs. We were a mixed bunch of colours: there were black and white kittens, ginger kittens, some with long hair, others with short hair, ginger and white kittens, a tortoise-shell, and me, a blonde cat with orange stripes, which of course makes me a very special tabby cat.

I think I made my mind up from the time that I could walk without falling over, that I was going to stay on the farm. Little kittens have to learn how to co-ordinate all four legs at the same time, which I can tell you takes some doing at first, but once we get the hang of it, we're up and away, jumping from one object to another.

As soon as I could walk without wobbling and run without falling, I would make my way over to the kind lady who came to the barn each day to feed us all, although I was more interested in climbing onto her knee and being made a fuss of, than the food she brought in. She called me Bo Jangles, and when my brothers and sisters were old enough to leave our mum and find new homes, I stayed. I think I must have woven myself into the human's heart. (We all call her that because we love her and she looks after us so well.)

It soon became very clear to all the other animals that live on the farm that I have very special, magical powers, because I can talk to them, and, to their surprise, they like talking to me too. I also know every hiding place on the farm, especially where the fairies live.

I make it my job to go around the farm each day to make sure everything is running as smoothly as possible. I like to think I'm doing my bit to help the human, although being curious by nature, it probably means I'm just being nosey.

Do you like dogs? Cats don't mind dogs at all; in fact, we like having them around so that we can tease them. We love them, really, as we like showing them who is the boss and of course, we are, because we are far smarter than they are. We walk around them with our tail and head in the air, that's the look of superiority, and to let them see how beautiful we are. We just like showing off. The big, big dog, Gem, is such a pushover we can walk right up to her, purring of course, and do our body rub, that's our way of saying hello, and she'll let us. In fact, she doesn't even attempt to move. I've even walked on her tail.

Anna, the little black dog, is fun because we can play with her. So, whatever you may have heard about dogs and cats not getting on is not true. Here on the farm, we all get on perfectly well because the dogs know their place and we're the boss. It's all about knowing who you are. If you believe you don't fit in, then you won't. If you believe everyone can play happily together, then everyone will get on. Cats believe they're better than dogs, so we win; it's as simple as that.

Now, I have to get out of the kitchen, but it's a little difficult at the moment, Gladys and her brood are here. Now you know what I was saying about cats and dogs, well, it doesn't work in quite the same way with mother hens and their brood of chicks.

You see, I know how to climb obstacles, that's what I do best; climbing trees, walking along rooftops, balancing on fences, you get the picture. I can jump up onto things and leap off from great heights, so I have nerves of steel, eyes like an eagle, great skills, and agility that can get me into and out of trouble. I'm very brave and very bright, too, because I have to learn very quickly around here that there are some things that I can and cannot do.

One thing I learned very quickly was that you do not even look at a mother hen with her brood of chicks. The beak of a hen is very powerful when used against the softness of a body. In other words, it hurts getting pecked, so I've learned that I have to show Gladys respect when I want to cross her path and not be attacked. The way I do that is with body language. You know, the way you hold yourself. When a cat holds its head up high, it's telling everyone that 'I'm the boss so don't mess with me.' But with Gladys I'm not the boss, she is, so to show her respect, I lower my head and drop my tail down to show her I have no intention of chasing her babies. By giving them a wide berth, putting as much space between us as I can, I'm free to walk away, unharmed. If however, I was to get it wrong, then she'd tell me off by running toward me with her beak ready to peck, giving me a painful reminder not to do it again.

Oh, and you know I told you about my nerves of steel and how confident I am at climbing trees and fences and all things high, because I was born to do that. Well, when it comes to walking past Gladys, I'm as weak as a kitten, because we don't speak the same language and I have to get my message across to her that I'm not going to hurt her or her babies. So, it was most important that I learned my lesson very quickly. I learned that you don't mess with something you're not sure of, especially a protective mother hen.

Right, here goes, head down, tail down, no looking and run. Phew! Made it! I'm safe now, so I'll continue to show you around the place. It's such a great place to grow up in, as you have to learn how to get around all the obstacles that can get in the way. I'm amazed at how much I have to learn each day. Take the day I had to learn how to use the cat flap so that I could come and go as I pleased. (I have to tell you that it's not exactly a cat flap in a door, it's an upstairs window we cats use to get into the house.) There are four cats, my mummy, Purdey, my auntie Izzie, and my cousin Lily, and we can come and go as we please as the kind human leaves this window open for us. It's just as well the cat flap isn't in the back door; otherwise the house would be invaded by Gladys and her chicks, as they just love coming into the kitchen to search for food. I think they're really after our biscuits.

Well, back to my tale, no, not my long tail, my short tale about how I learned to use the upstairs window. Getting in wasn't so difficult, I had to use my claws to climb up a post and walk across the wooden plank, which was easy, then I had to jump up onto the kitchen roof and run up to the top, then balance myself until I was ready to make the big jump onto a narrow window sill. I stretched my body until I could put my claws into the window frame so that I didn't slip, then pulled myself up to the little window that was open, then I was in. It took a bit of doing at first, but I soon got the hang of it and the human was very kind, because when I needed to go outside, she would open the back door for me. Jumping down wasn't so easy, as when I sat on the window frame looking down, I got scared and my body shook. For a little fellah like me, it looked an awful long way down and what if I missed the roof, I'd fall and hurt myself. I was very worried, because even though I know that cats are very special and can bounce quite well, I didn't want to fall and hurt myself.

I guess you're wondering why I have to learn how to leap in and out of the upstairs window. Well, it all began when Mummy Purdy and her sister Izzie arrived at the farm as kittens. Being as inquisitive as they were, one day while exploring their new surroundings they found an open window. Curiosity got the better of them, and they climbed through it and found this wonderful, warm, cosy house which was full of rooms to hide in, and they thought it was a much better place to live in than a cold barn. Because of the dogs that lived in the house, they used this window as a means of getting in and out without disturbing them. My mummy told me it was quite a while before the human or the dogs knew that they'd made themselves at home and were sleeping in the house. They'd hide themselves under beds or behind doors, wherever they liked really because no one stopped them.

Eventually, the dogs got used to them and the human left the window open on purpose so they always had a means of getting in and out, especially if she wasn't around. My mummy told me I had to learn this lesson, otherwise I would have to stay out in the cold barn, and the thought of a cold night shivering didn't seem very appealing, especially as I'd got so use to the warmth. So my only option now was to learn how to jump in and out of the window like the other cats. For days I went to the window and looked out. I sat there trying to convince myself that I could do it, but each time I looked down, I went all funny and floppy. My nerves got the better of me; I couldn't do it. Shall I tell you what I learned from this lesson?

By going to the window and looking down, I learned that we all have limitations, sometimes we just have to wait until we're big enough or old enough to try certain things. Of course, without knowing it, each day that I went to the window I'd grown a little more, we kittens grow very quickly, so it wasn't too long before the drop didn't look so scary. Of course, by going to the window each day, it began to look more and more familiar. It also gave me the time to work out how to make the jump, instead of just thinking I could do it. This lesson taught me that in life you have to think about a problem in order to solve it. I found that working out my route was fun. It was much safer trying out the different routes I could take in my head, than flying through the air to find no roof beneath me. Each day that I sat at the window looking out, not only did my shaking get less and less, but my confidence grew, because it all felt more and more familiar. You see, sometimes we think we can't do these things because we're not really ready to try them and when we know this and we stop worrying, we can become more relaxed about it. I stopped worrying about what I couldn't do and concentrated instead on what I knew I could do. I knew that I could jump up and down, onto and off the fences. I knew that my claws were sharp enough to climb the trees, but my muscles were not strong enough to get me all the way to the top, as I was still a kitten; but, I also knew it was only a matter of time before I'd be big enough to tackle the biggest tree on the farm.

It took about a week of going to the window and looking out to get less and less worried and scared and more and more confident; I planned my route and saw it all in my head until it happened, not by chance, but because I felt ready to try it. I had rehearsed it so many times that I knew what to do. I kept my cool, took my time, and when it felt right, my body was relaxed and I took that leap, with my front legs out in front, ready for the landing. I landed softly. I was so excited that I'd done the first part successfully. The next part was much easier as I had to run up the roof, over the top, jump down onto the lower roof, take another leap, and then I was on the ground. The way down was slightly different to going up, but it felt so good doing it. Then I went back again. I ran up the post along the plank, jumped onto the roof, ran up the roof, made that leap onto the window sill, and in through the window, mission accomplished. I'd done it.

I did that circuit so many times, each time I got better and better at it, so that when night time came, I knew I would be able to do it in the dark, as I now felt so confident. I knew where to land and where to take off. But even though I knew I could do it, I had to keep practicing until I felt safe, sure-footed, and really confident. I was so happy I could hold my head up high and walk like a grown-up. That night I slept in the house, knowing that when the sun began to rise and the sky began to lighten, I could go out hunting with my mummy instead of being left behind, which had always made me feel sad. I was now nearly a grown-up cat and my mummy could teach me how to hunt for myself, which would be great fun.

Misty Blue

On a bright, sunny, winter's day, I was on my usual routine tour around the farm, when I just happened to stop and listen to a conversation between Charlie Buttons, the spotted pony, and Tiger Tom, the miniature Shetland.

"Did you see what that Misty did?" Tiger asked Charlie while they stood warming themselves in the winter sunshine. It felt so good to feel the warmth of the sun on our backs.

"No, I didn't actually see him going mad, jumping everything in sight, I missed it, but, I did hear about it. Silly horse, he does make life difficult sometimes," Charlie said with a look of disapproval on his face. "I honestly think Misty Blue makes life quite difficult for everyone on purpose."

"What do you mean, Charlie?" Tiger asked with a puzzled look on his face.

"He rubs the human up the wrong way," replied Charlie.

"Explain a little more, will you? I'm not being thick, I just want to make sure that we're both thinking the same thing," said Tiger to Charlie. It was a good conversation to have while they both enjoyed the sunshine, a bit like two men talking about the weather while watching a game of cricket, keeping one eye on the match, while the other was sort of trying to stay awake.

"He just doesn't get the game," said Charlie, trying to explain himself.

"What game?" Tiger asked, as his ears moved forward, not wanting to miss a word. "I think that's always been the trouble with Misty, he plays too many games and the poor human always seems to end up being the loser."

"The game of life," replied Charlie in a manner that suggested he thought that everyone knew about the game of life.

"I don't think I know that one, could you explain the rules to me?" asked Tiger.

"Certainly, it would be my pleasure, seeing as I'm a little older and therefore wiser than you," Charlie replied with a slight snigger in his voice. "You see, we all have to get along together, like one big, happy family, even though we're not. The fact that we live here, all together, as a herd means that we should all get along."

"Yep, I get that," replied Tiger. "I also know about the pecking order, in that someone has to be top horse and someone has to be at the bottom and then there are the ones in between, but I think you're trying to say something different, aren't you?"

"Yes, I am," said Charlie, "and, if you'll let me finish, I will explain further. Misty seems to think he can do just what he likes and get away with it. I know he thinks he's so clever at being able to jump the fences and gallop around the field, showing off. I'm not moaning about that. It's the other things he does that upset me. He doesn't seem to understand that when he upsets the human, we all suffer."

"Go on," urged Tiger, wanting to know more. "I know I'm only a little pony, which means that I'm way down the line when it comes to being important in Misty's eyes."

"I've watched him, in fact, I've studied him," Charlie continued. "As soon as he sees the human approaching with a head collar and lead rope, he clenches his jaw and puts his hooves down into the ground. He's already made up his mind that he's not going to move. He doesn't seem to mind having the head collar put on, it's when the human pulls on the lead rope that his objection begins. All she wants to do with him is take him for a walk. That's not too difficult, is it? To Misty, you'd think she was asking him to work."

"What does he do then?" asked Tiger.

"Nothing, that's the problem," continued Charlie, his nostrils beginning to flare a little as he got more annoyed describing Misty's antics to Tiger. "He just stands there and defies the human. He looks down his nose at her, stares her out, and refuses to move his hooves in a forward direction. I've seen her make him go backwards and sideways, which he'll do just to annoy her even more. I've even seen him go around and around in circles, and he's pretty good at those. In fact, he's very impressive when he's playing her up, but forwards is a definite *no, no*. You can see the human getting more and more upset by his refusal to move. All she's asking him to do is to walk forwards. The more he refuses, the redder she gets in the face. You'd think he'd have worked it out by now, that he uses far more energy in not going forwards, but he's just plain stubborn and won't move an inch, unless, of course, the human bribes him to move with some tasty treat in the hope that he'll place one hoof in front of the other in order to get it."

"Does it work?" Tiger asked. "Maybe I could try it now and again, you know, to see if the human would give me some tasty treats in order to get me to move. The only problem is I'm usually so eager to please her, that it never crosses my mind to be awkward or stubborn."

"Oh yes! It works for Misty. He's got it off to a fine art. One day though, mark my words, he'll push her too far," Charlie replied with a stern look on his face.

"What do you reckon she'll do?" Tiger asked with a worried look on his face. "I've seen the human shout at Misty and always wondered what had caused such a reaction in her, as she is normally so quiet and calm. I guess sometimes things happen that upset her more than other times."

"I guess they do," Charlie replied with a look on his face and a roll of his eyes that made me smile.

I was finding this all so interesting, as I sat there following the conversation between Charlie and Tiger. Some days I got to hear the most interesting of stories, and of course, I always liked to keep my ears pricked for any news that might be flying around; after all I had a job to do—I was the man, well young cat really, who liked to help wherever I could.

"Maybe we could have a word with him and see if he could ease up a little and start to cooperate with her a little more, that way we all win. I mean, it's only a suggestion," Tiger offered as I watched Charlie roll his eyes again in disbelief.

"Do you really think he would listen to us? He never ever talks to us, he just looks down his nose at us as he passes by, so, do you really think we could go up to him and say, look here dear chap, do you think you could?" Charlie said with a slight edge to his voice. You could tell he wasn't happy with Misty Blue, but I guess he was afraid to say something, just in case he took it the wrong way.

"Yeah, I get your point, but I do know who he would listen to," Tiger said with more optimism in his voice.

"You do? Who?" asked Charlie, taken aback by Tiger's remark.

"Tilly. She adores him, and he lets her graze right next to him, which means he must like her, as he accepts her in his space," Tiger said with pride, knowing his daughter could be the one that saved the day.

"Brilliant idea! I'll leave you to say something to her," Charlie said as he began to walk away.

"Hang on a minute! Don't walk away. You need to tell me

what to say," Tiger pleaded as he desperately tried to keep up with Charlie, whose legs were a lot longer than his.

"It's time to eat. You'll figure something out, I know you will," Charlie replied as he began to munch on the green shoots of grass that just happened to be close by.

"I just needed to get that off my chest, Bo. Did you hear it all?" Charlie asked as he gave a sideways glance in my direction.

"I did. It was so interesting. Why don't you say something to Misty if you think he's being nasty?" I asked Charlie, looking him straight in the eye. I knew he loved his Shetlands and the way Misty treated everyone, especially the human, had obviously been bothering him.

"It's no good, Bo," Charlie said, dropping his head down a little closer to the ground so that he could see me. "I'm no good against the bigger horses, they just don't respect me, and to be honest, I'm a little scared of them, so I stay out of their way."

"Maybe it's your spots they don't like," I offered as a way of an explanation.

Charlie laughed. "I don't think it has anything to do with my spots, Bo. Unfortunately, Misty knows I can't stand up to him, so he doesn't respect me. There's nothing I can do except stay out of his way. I can't change my appearance, but I could be braver. Only I think I'm a little too old to change now. I know the human is usually there to help me when things get tough. Feeding times are the most difficult, as it seems to bring the worst out in all the bigger horses. Now you know why she is so special to me, and why I don't like seeing her upset. I do hope Tilly can sort that Misty out," Charlie said with a tear in his eye, which I could just see as it glistened in the sunlight.

"Don't worry, Charlie," I said in the best reassuring voice I could find. "I'm sure Tilly will do her best. I'll go and find out what's happening."

"That's a good idea, Bo. You're a good boy keeping a watchful eye on everyone. Off you go now, while I have a little nap in this lovely sunshine. It feels mighty good on my back," Charlie said as his eyelids began to close.

"Okay, Charlie, see you later," I shouted back at him, knowing it was time for me to go and find Tiger and see if he'd managed to have a word with Tilly.

Now it was Tiger's turn to do something to help the herd. You see, everyone has a role to play, even though some don't seem as important as others, but, actually, they all count. Tiger may have been a tiny Shetland pony, but he was big in character, and to his family he was very important. Now he needed to find his daughter, Tilly, because the whole herd needed her help. Even though the big ones might not think it, everyone was affected by Misty's behaviour. You see, the one causing the problem never sees what they leave behind; they're too busy walking away. It's a bit like a big wave that washes up onto the beach: it's so big that everyone has to run out of its way to reach safety. As the wave crashes down, it disturbs all the sand and pebbles, even destroying the beautiful sandcastles that the children have been so happy and busy building, and then it rolls back down the beach and into the sea. The wave comes and goes without worrying about the effect it has; the only thing it knows is that it is going to roll up onto the beach and then roll back again.

So you see, when someone misbehaves like Misty does, he doesn't really care about what he does. He just likes doing things to please himself and doesn't worry that it might cause upset to the others, because he thinks it's funny, especially when he can make the human feel uncomfortable. Unfortunately, he gets away with it because no one wants to tell him the truth; they don't want to upset him, even though he upsets them. He hasn't worked out that the human feeds him and looks after all his other needs and all she asks in return is for him to cooperate. Now, that isn't too much to ask, is it?

"Hang on, Tiger," I shouted as I ran after him. "Can I come with you to find Tilly? This is all so interesting that I don't want to miss a thing."

"I suppose so," Tiger said with a hint of sadness in his voice. "I don't really know what to do or say. You couldn't help me could you, Bo?"

"Me, help you?" I replied. Well that stopped me in my tracks, I can tell you. A young cat like me helping. "Well if you think I can be of help, I'll do my best."

"Hop on board then. Let's go and find Tilly," Tiger suggested, sounding much happier. I liked riding on Tiger's back; it was great fun and so exciting feeling the wind ruffling my fur. Tiger's coat was so thick I knew I couldn't hurt him as I clung on using my sharp claws, as I didn't fancy falling off.

"There she is over there by the big oak tree," I shouted into Tiger's ears so that he could hear me. Standing on top of his back meant I had a better view of the field and could see much farther. "She's standing with Misty."

"Oh no, what are we going to do now?" Tiger gasped, stopping a little too abruptly, as I gambolled over his head and landed in a heap in front of his hooves.

Picking myself up and doing the body roll to get my fur back into place, I looked directly into his eyes, puffed myself up as big as I could, and then said in my loudest and strongest voice, "You're going to walk right over there and talk to your daughter. She'll look after you." Then almost as an afterthought, I whispered to Tiger, "You've never been afraid of Misty have you?"

"I'm sorry to say, Bo, but I have been many times," Tiger whispered back, as if afraid of being over heard. "Monty and Tilly don't seem to be scared of him at all. In fact, they like playing with him, but I'm like Charlie, I stay out of his way as much as I can, because he worries me. He has a certain look which makes me feel very small."

"Don't be scared, Tiger. Everything will be fine. You can trust us younger ones to know just what to do. Come on," I said, leading the way. Suddenly I felt all big and brave, so I ran ahead and got to Tilly first, whispering to her so that Misty couldn't hear. I asked her to walk toward her dad as he wanted a word in her ear.

"Sure," Tilly said as she started walking. "Do you know what he wants, Bo?" she asked all bouncy and happy. I like Tilly because she's always so friendly and quite cuddly. She looks like a big creamy coloured powder puff on four little legs. She's a little cutie and she knows it.

"Tilly, we need you to do something very important," Tiger blurted out. "We need you to talk to Misty. Explain to him that it takes less time and energy to be good and do as he's asked the first time, instead of being so awkward and uncooperative and upsetting the human."

"Wow, Dad, you don't want much do you?" Tilly looked at Tiger and then down at me.

"You've got to do something, Tilly." Tiger took a step closer to his daughter. "He'll listen to you. He likes you, and besides, Charlie said we have to do something because the human is upset. He saw her crying."

"Okay, Dad, don't get upset. I'll do my best, but don't hold your breath," Tilly said as she walked away. I could tell she was on a mission by the way she was walking, head forwards looking directly at Misty.

I ran after her and caught up with her just before she got to Misty. "It's really important that you get him to understand, Tilly. It's not just about him, as everyone is affected by his behaviour, especially, when he upsets the human. We all depend on her to feed and care for us. So please do your best." I used my best voice on her, the one with a slight tremble and a long, loud purr as I wove myself in and out of her little legs, just to get my point across.

"I will, Bo. I promise," she said as she looked down at me. "I know how important it is. I will try my hardest to get him to listen, but I'm not promising anything."

As she headed off towards Misty, I knew not to follow her even though my nose was twitching with curiosity—that's what cats are renowned for. My curiosity gets me into many interesting places, and sometimes it gets me into trouble. Trouble wasn't something I was looking for today, but I could tell by Misty's body language, and the way his ears were moving back and forth, that he was listening to what Tilly had to say, but would he take any notice of her? I stayed watching them until Tilly made her way back over to me.

"Well, I've done my best, Bo. He said he'd think about it. We just have to wait and see if he changes. I told him that he had to consider everyone else in the herd and that when he was unkind to the human, we all suffered."

"Well done, Tilly. I think it was very brave of you. Thanks for trying. I'm sure he'll want to help his friends," I said in my reassuring voice, trying to convince myself as much as Tilly. Maybe Misty could change his spots and his ways, we'll just have to wait and see. Fingers, toes, paws and hooves crossed.

The Penny Drops with Misty

Down on the farm, everyone was quietly going about their own business. It was still winter, so it was important to eat as much as they could, to lay down the layers of fat that they needed in order to keep warm on those cold winter days and nights, in much the same way that you put on extra clothes and heavy coats. You see, the animals on the farm don't live in nice, warm, cosy houses like humans and they don't wrap themselves up in blankets or fleeces, coats or jackets. Instead, Mother Nature provides them with a nice, thick fur coat and a layer of fat that helps them to stay warm and dry during the cold winter months.

Jack Frost was a regular visitor in winter and left an icy, white trail behind him. The horses quite liked his visits, because he made the grass a little sweeter to eat, and they really loved the snow. Even though they couldn't build snowmen like humans, or have snowball fights, they just loved playing in the snow. Chasing one another around was great fun, and it helped to keep them warm. The ponies knew that when winter arrived, they didn't have much time for their usual games, because they needed to save their energy and keep warm. Even Misty knew that this wasn't the time for his usual playful frolics, or maybe there was another reason for his quiet behaviour.

I wonder if Tilly's quiet word helped. Do you think it's time

17

to find out? Let's go and find Tiger and Charlie and see what they have to say. They must be around here somewhere. First, we'll look in the barn where the hay is stacked. No, they're not there, and I can't see them in the fields, either; they must be hiding somewhere. Oh, there they are, behind the barn, sheltered from the wind with their own pile of hay.

"Ah ha! Found you both. It looks nice and cosy here, tucked away from the big horses," I said with a pleased look on my face. I like it when I find what I'm looking for. Nothing escapes me.

"Yes," Charlie replied, trying to speak with a mouthful of hay. "We like it here knowing that we can eat our hay in peace and quiet."

"Have you any news, anything to report?" I asked, all excited.

"What news?" Charlie asked between mouthfuls.

"Well, I was wondering if you'd had the help you needed in sorting the Misty problem out," I enquired, hopeful that something had happened.

"Oh yes, it was strange, really. Would you like me to tell you?" Charlie asked, knowing that he was teasing me.

"Of course we want you to tell us," Tiger and I replied together. We were all ears.

"Well," Charlie continued, "this nice young girl came along the other day and walked right up to him, and then started talking very firmly to him."

"Do you think the human asked her to come?" I asked, my little pink nose and ears twitching at the excitement of it all.

"I don't really know, she just appeared," Charlie replied.

"How do you know what she told him?" I asked. Cats are renowned for their curiosity, and I am definitely one of those cats who has curiosity written all over me, right down to the very tip of my tail.

"Come on, Charlie! There's more to tell," Tiger butted in.

"There is, if you two will just give me a minute," Charlie said as he caught his breath. Making himself comfortable, he gave a little cough as if to clear his throat. "That's better," he continued. "Well, it just so happens that a friend of mine observed the whole proceedings with Misty and the young girl, and assured me that, from Misty's body language, he wasn't happy with what he was hearing. You know his behaviour is not unlike that of some humans. It's well-known that humans can have these stubborn streaks or tendencies where they think they know best, even when they don't. Even though they're not aware of it at the time, they lose out on the fun of the circus, so to speak."

"What do you mean?" I asked, eager to know more. Getting a little closer, I made myself more comfortable on the sweet-smelling pile of hay that Charlie had been eating from, as I didn't want to miss a word.

"Well," Charlie grunted, "if I might be allowed to continue. They're so blind to what's going on around them, because they're so focused on what they want, that they miss out on so much more, especially fun. Of course, they think they're in control, but they're not really, their emotions are."

"Is that true?" Tiger asked, looking a little bewildered. "I always thought Misty was a complicated chap."

"Yes," Charlie continued. "You see, stubbornness isn't something you see or feel. It doesn't hurt, so there's no pain. Stubborn people don't usually like looking at themselves, either. They don't see what everyone else sees."

"Wait a moment! I thought you said you couldn't see stubbornness. I'm confused," I said, looking over to see that poor Tiger was looking just as confused as I was.

"I meant that it's something the stubborn person chooses not to recognise about himself or herself. Everyone around them can see the real person, the one that isn't cooperative or helpful or funny, only no one says anything, because they don't want to upset them or hurt them. Well, according to my friend who was standing very close by and able to watch it all without being observed, it was amazing to see Misty just standing there listening.

"Unfortunately, she couldn't hear everything that was being said, but thought that from his body language, the way he stood with his head lowered down, it looked as if this young girl was telling him some home truths. Then, she heard her shout at him, 'if you don't like it, go!' But Misty being Misty stayed, and when she told him 'to change his attitude or else,' he stomped his feet, which was just so typical of Misty, and then she left."

"So, what worked? Something must have happened to change him," I asked quite boldly, knowing that everyone had seen and felt the change in Misty, so something had happened, but this was the first time anyone had really spoken about it. Maybe they were all frightened that if they talked about it, the new Misty would leave and the old one would come back.

"If I may?" Charlie coughed.

Looking directly at me, I saw a little twinkle in his eye and a hint of a smile on his lips. I knew he was really enjoying himself, so it was my turn to tease him a little. "Yes, please do, we're all ears," I sniggered, as both Tiger and I moved our ears back and forth, which of course made Charlie laugh.

"Well," he continued, trying his hardest not to look at us as we continued to twitch our ears trying to make him laugh. "Apparently the others had come to see what was happening, and with an audience watching, Misty wasn't going to give in so easily. He knew that his little flare-ups disturbed the peace, but he was only playing, which is what he usually told everyone. It was then that something happened, which took him completely by surprise. All the big horses turned away from him."

"They didn't," I choked, trying to get my words out.

"Yes, they did. They actually turned their backs on him and even worse—they walked away and left him on his own. It's what he deserved," Charlie said with a slight edge to his voice.

"Wow! That was powerful," I said, knowing that what Misty's friends had done would have a big effect on him. Sometimes words aren't necessary, because the body's language says so much more. In this case, Misty knew exactly what they'd all said to him: "enough is enough." I guess his stubbornness was no longer the friend he thought it was. Although he thought he was the playful joker, none of the others liked this part of his character and they showed him that day how they really felt by walking away.

"Apparently," Charlie continued, puffing himself up even more, "Misty stood there quite perplexed, as if he didn't know what to do next. Being stubborn and showing off were parts of his character. Not doing what the big human asked was his way of saying he was in charge. It didn't matter to him that he made her cry and hurt her feelings; he didn't care. He still got fed and a clean stable to lay down in. He didn't even have to worry about being ridden or being made to do things he didn't like, because as far as he was concerned, she couldn't hurt him. But standing there alone, with no audience to play to, wouldn't have felt the same, and suddenly he would have felt the pain of not being liked. My guess is that was the moment when he knew he had to change."

"How do you know so much, Charlie?" I asked.

"Because I know what it feels like, Bo, when someone doesn't like you. It hurts."

"Charlie, we love you," Tiger piped in, all emotional, walking up to him and putting his head against Charlie's shoulder.

"I know, Tiger, thank you." I could hear the emotion in

Charlie's voice as he looked down at his friend with softness in his eyes and a slight tilt of his head. "You and your family are very precious to me, and I'll always do the best I can to look after you all," Charlie gulped.

"But what happened to Misty?" I asked, wanting to know more.

"I don't know, Bo," Charlie said wiping the tears away from his eyes. "You'll have to go and ask him yourself."

"Me? Ask Misty?"

"Yes, Bo. You don't have a problem talking to us, so just walk up to him and start talking."

"But Misty isn't like you and Tiger."

"You have nothing to lose by trying, Bo, and everything to gain by asking."

"You're right, Charlie. I'll do it. All I have to do is find him."

"Then off you go, Bo, and leave me and Tiger to enjoy our hay in peace."

I trotted off and searched for him thinking that he'd be in the field with the others, only he wasn't. Eventually I found him all alone in the big barn. I puffed myself up so that I looked like a bigger, older cat, and walked straight up to him. "Hi, Misty, nice day," I said feeling very confident in myself.

"Who said that?" Misty replied, sounding a little shocked.

"It's me, Bo. I'm down here by your hooves."

"Come out where I can see you," Misty said with a quiver in his voice. "Oh! It's you, Bo. I thought it was that voice again. I couldn't see you down there."

"What voice?" I asked, holding my breath, as I had a feeling that this was going to be very interesting.

"Well, Bo, it's all a bit strange really, but this voice started talking to me. It seemed to come out of the wall. It happened the other day just after that young girl left me standing there all alone wondering what to do next. I felt embarrassed and ashamed of my behaviour, when this loud, clear voice told me to change my ways 'or else'?

"Then the voice grew much softer as it told me not to worry. All I had to do was to stop pretending to be someone I wasn't. The penny dropped as I began to understand what it was trying to tell me. I realised that all this time I'd been playing a game, pretending I was so important and thinking that everyone enjoyed it when I showed off and played up, but really, they were only putting up with me because I didn't give them a choice."

My curiosity was growing by the second. This was all so interesting, my little pink nose and ears were twitching, and even my tail had decided to join in, too.

"Are you really interested in my story, Bo?" Misty asked.

As he looked down at me, I caught a glimpse of a softness that I never thought Misty had. Perhaps it was because I'd never given him a chance; I'd always believed what everyone else said about him.

"I am, Misty. Really I am. Please continue," I replied, eager for more.

"I was pretty cross at first, getting all hot and prickly, as it's not nice having to listen while someone says things about you that you'd rather not hear, but at the same time I knew that what the voice was telling me was true. It all made sense.

"I learned from the voice that I only pretended to be the joker, as I didn't want my friends to see the real Misty—the one who sometimes feels nervous or afraid, confused or worried, as I thought they wouldn't like that Misty. So I created a character I thought they would like, only they didn't. And I know I pushed the human to her limits, but most of the time it was because there was an audience, and I didn't want to let them see I was really a big, soft chap who wanted to be loved."

"So what are you going to do now, Misty? Did the voice give you some advice?" I asked, suddenly seeing him in a new light. He wasn't so bad after all. He just didn't know that his behaviour wasn't to everyone's liking, especially as no one had bothered to tell him he wasn't always as funny as he thought he was. Just then, I caught a glimpse of something white out of the corner of my eye, but I didn't want to appear rude, so I let Misty continue with his tale.

"I'm trying my hardest to remember to not get all hot and prickly when something upsets me. The voice told me to think first before I say or do something I'll regret, so I've made up a little ditty to help me. Would you like to hear it, Bo?"

"Yes please, I'd be honoured," I said as I sat there stroking my whiskers, slightly embarrassed to have his undivided attention, but it was obvious to me that Misty had been doing a lot of thinking and working things out as to how he could improve himself. The least I could do now was to give him the opportunity to show off the new Misty, the one that everyone was going to like.

Holding his head up high Misty began. "Do I want prickles or a fine smooth coat? Shall I play with friends or stand all alone? Should I be the joker, the clown, or a fine friend to know?"

And do you know, Bo, that by the time I've asked myself those questions, whatever was troubling me has gone. The moment has passed, and I'm back to being the nice, easy-going person that everyone likes. I'm not angry, confused, or uncomfortable anymore."

"That's very impressive, Misty. I must say that when I do my rounds, looking and listening to everything that's going on, I have noticed the change. It's a much happier place and everyone seems more settled."

"I know," Misty replied, obviously feeling very pleased with himself as he began to smile. "We're living in harmony where everything feels smooth and round, no sharp edges or ruffles that make you feel uneasy or disturbed. It's a place of nice colours, like the rainbow in the sky, which brings a smile to your face and makes you feel good inside. So from now on, I'm going to be nice and considerate to everyone, even Charlie and Tiger and especially the human. I'm not going to be so stubborn when she asks me to walk on, and I'll try my hardest not to upset her anymore."

"I'm pleased to hear it, Misty, and I know they'll be pleased, too. Everyone can live in harmony with one another as long as we all make the effort."

"I'm off now, Bo, and thanks for listening, it's been a great help," and with that he disappeared round the corner trotting off to find his friends, all excited and happy. I knew he had a lot of explaining to do, but he also had a lot of playing to catch up with, too, only this time they'd all be playing happily together, as one big happy family.

Now that he was gone, I needed to find Tilly. Fortunately, I didn't have to look too far as she was hanging around outside, eavesdropping. "Hi, Tilly. May I ask you a really important question?"

"I suppose so," she responded in a coy sort of way, as if she already knew what I was going to ask her.

"Were you the voice Misty heard through the wall?" I asked, so sure that my detective nose had been right on the button, so to speak. "In case you don't want to admit it, I would like to thank you for doing such an excellent job."

"You won't tell anyone, will you, Bo?" she asked as she looked me directly in the eye.

"Your secret is safe with me," I assured her as I wove in and out of her legs purring in my best voice. Tilly really had saved the day.

No one talked of the change in Misty; they didn't have to.

They were all too busy enjoying his company. Even the human appeared more settled. No longer ruffled by his behaviour, she just called his name and he trotted towards her. Everyone was so happy now, but no one more than Misty Blue, as he no longer had to show off just to get their attention.

Oh! How Naughty Can They Be?

Down on the farm on a beautiful sunny morning, there was something different in the air, you could feel it. It made my fur tingle, it was excitement. As always, news travels fast around here and this day was no exception. We were expecting the arrival of two new animals – two piglets by all accounts; well, so I heard.

You know how it goes? Gem and Anna had heard it directly from the human. Apparently she'd fallen in love with these two little squealers. These little piglets were bright orange, black, and white and had spots too, large black ones, quite a sight to behold, me-thinks.

Well, Anna and Gem told Gladys, the chicken, whilst she was sitting upon her nest of straw, laying her egg, who told Purdey, my mum, and while deep in conversation about yesterday's events, Gladys let it slip that these new arrivals were on their way, this very day. Purdey, of course, ran off to tell her sister, Izzie, who was just about to catch a squirrel, ha, ha; they were always too quick, but it never stopped her from trying; and of course, the squirrel immediately ran off with the news, telling Eddie, the owl, and Colin, the crow and so on. Meanwhile, Purdey and Izzie spread the news to the ponies, who in turn told the horses, so you can imagine the size of the crowd who came to see the piglets arrive. They all stood there waiting patiently, it

27

was a little like waiting for royalty to arrive, as there were lots of great whoops and cheers as everyone was in high spirits waiting for their arrival.

The moment came; a trailer arrived and pulled into the field opposite the main yard. These piglets had had a run specially built for them, because they don't live in stables like horses; their homes are called sties and the one the human had built them was more like a little wooden house; it even had curtains at the windows to keep the sun off their bodies, because, get this, pigs can get sunburned.

We all stood there watching, waiting for these little piglets to come running out of the trailer. The dogs stood in readiness, in case they needed to chase them. Well, who knows? We waited and waited and nothing happened; apparently they'd gone to sleep and were curled up in the straw, snoring. The human didn't want to disturb them, but we were all so excited and wanted to see them. The horses stood frozen to the spot, their eyes glued to the back of the trailer, ready for any sign of movement. Eventually, the piglets walked out; they were totally unaware of all the fuss they'd created. It was as if they were walking on the red carpet, showing themselves off to their adoring fans. They stood for a moment, looking around and taking everything in, and on seeing such a large crowd of animals all waiting and watching every move they made, they went and did something. Can you guess what they did? They ran off. Those naughty, little, orange, black, and white piglets took everyone by surprise and ran. They weren't running away, they were playing. Well, the horses couldn't believe their eyes. "Loose pigs," they shouted.

Annie ran off in a panic thinking that they might eat her, or so she told the ponies later on. The little ponies thought this was a great game, as they joined in, chasing after the big horses, until it looked like a race track, with everyone leaping and jumping in the air and running around in circles. Misty showed off by jumping the fences, any excuse for having fun. The horses and ponies just loved running after one another and playing tag; it was their way of showing how good they felt.

The birds had all flapped their wings and flown up into the nearest tree to keep out of the way, and also to get a better view of the proceedings that were continuing. Pigs, you know, can run quite fast, and like the ponies, they can weave in and out of things, especially legs, very quickly. The dogs thought this was great fun, too, and were barking and chasing these little piglets that were having such a good time. They squealed and whooped in delight. The humans didn't know what to do, for as much as they ran after them, they just couldn't succeed in catching them. These little piglets were far too clever. It was really funny seeing humans throw themselves onto the ground, in the hope that as they scooped their arms together, there might just be a piglet between them when they landed face down in the grass. My sides were aching from laughing so much, watching the antics of these new arrivals. They had already brought so much joy and happiness to the farm. I had a funny feeling that things might never be quite the same again.

Like all baby animals, after a while they had to stop, especially after so much exertion, so it wasn't too long before they stood panting, waiting for the human to arrive, with, can you guess what, a bucket of food.

"Oh boy!" the piglets squealed in unison.

"This is going to be a great place to live," said Plumpkin, the larger piglet, to her sister, Penelope. "And how easy is this human going to be to train?" she said with a rather smug smile on her face, as her head quickly disappeared into the bucket of food being held out in front of them both. The human was asking them to follow her and the food, which of course, they did, as they were such obedient and good little girls.

Their run was a nice area of dirt with lots of roots to dig for and their pig sty was a lovely wooden house with curtains at the windows and door and a lovely thick carpet of straw for them to lay on. This was heaven, a perfect place for them to live, they were going to be very happy here and they were going to have lots of fun training the human.

Everything settled down, the horses and ponies had all stopped running around and now stood contentedly grazing. The birds had flown off to other trees, and Sammy, the squirrel, had gone back to his dray for a sleep. "Too much excitement for one," he said as he settled himself down. The human stood watching Plumpkin and Penelope as they settled themselves down, too, making their beds in the nice, thick straw, as it was time for sleep.

A good day had been had by all, everyone had enjoyed themselves and now all that could be heard was the soft, contented sounds of sleep: a gentle grunt, a soft purr, a tiny snort and sniff, a little gasp; all the animals on the farm, no matter whether they were standing or lying, curled up in a ball or stretched out, were all lost in their own inner world of sleep, their eyes tightly closed, shutting the outside world completely out. Maybe they were even reliving the events of this enjoyable day.

Annie Meets Plumpkin

Once upon a day down on the farm, it was decided that the horses and ponies were to be moved into the field next to the pigs. This was perhaps not the best decision that was made as normally pigs and horses don't really mix. However, it turned out to be a very good move for one horse in particular. It was interesting to watch as the horses made their way over to the fence to watch the pigs busy eating their breakfast. Being the brave and inquisitive cat that I am, I was safely out of their way, lying along a branch on a very tall tree.

"Hi everyone, my name is Annie, and I know I'm very beautiful, and I'm a very clean and tidy horse."

"Where did that come from?" asked Plumpkin, looking around as she tried to find out who would say such a thing.

"It's me," said Annie.

"Who's me?" asked Plumpkin, unable to see very well because her very big ears flopped over her eyes and prevented her from seeing things unless they were right in front of her, like the food she was eating. Her poor eyesight never stopped her from being naughty, though.

"Tell me where you are and I'll find you," yelled Plumpkin, hoping that whoever it was would hear her. She was now on a mission; she wanted to find out who it was that wanted to talk to her and who thought herself so beautiful.

"I'm over here by the fence," replied Annie, her nose in the air as she tried not to smell the piggy smells coming from the other side of the fence.

"I've found you. Whoa, I didn't think you'd be that big," Plumpkin spoke, as she lifted her head in order to see the big, brown horse standing by the fence. "Well, don't you look just fine and you are pretty, too. How come you want to speak to me? I didn't think you big horses liked us smelly, dirty pigs."

"Well, normally we don't," replied Annie, "but I wanted to thank you, because you've helped me so much."

"Me helped you, but how? This is the first time we've met," said Plumpkin.

"I know, but you've helped me every day to overcome my fears," Annie said, as she stood looking over the fence at this strange-looking animal, which appeared to be so much bigger now that she was so close to her.

"Go on, I'm listening, you have my full attention." Plumpkin was really listening now. Normally she was so busy doing her own thing that she didn't hear anything, well, she made out she couldn't hear, but somehow she always heard the rattle of a bucket, that always managed to get her full attention.

Sometimes, she would run to the gate in her field just to scare the horses, because she knew they didn't really like pigs. All that separated them was a narrow road, and occasionally she would stand on her back legs so that they could see her head and then she'd call out to them. She wasn't always sure if they understood her, but the look on their faces was enough to make her day. Being a rather large, orange coloured pig with black spots made her quite a sight. In fact, to some horses, she was quite a frightening sight, and when she was being very naughty, she always got her sister to join in, too, that way it was double trouble.

"Well," Annie began, "when you and your sister arrived, we

all wondered what you would look like, but you were so far away that we couldn't really see you that well. So every day, I would imagine what you looked like. I knew you were small, so I had little images of you both running around like the dogs that visit us every day. That wasn't too bad at first, because I was in control of my images. Then you started to grow. I saw you when you escaped and ran across the field and I began to worry. I worried that you would escape and get into my field and chase me. Then I imagined you growing and growing, getting sooooo big that you'd eat me. Every day, I kept looking over the fence toward your field in the hope of seeing you both, so that I could scare myself even more. It was silly really, because the more I thought about you, the more I scared myself. The more I needed to see you in order to make sure you were still there and hadn't escaped, the more I scared myself into believing that you could escape and you'd come and eat me. The images in my head grew until it hurt and I knew I wasn't in control anymore."

"So, what happened?" asked Plumpkin. "What made you stop being scared of us?"

"Well," Annie continued, "one day, I stood looking at you, with my nerves all jangling together. I was in a terrible state. I could feel myself shaking inside. My ears were as tall as I could make them, pointing them towards you so that I could hear where you were. You see, our ears are like radar, they pick up tiny movements and sounds. My eyes were open so wide, my nostrils were flared, my legs were dancing on the spot, and my coat was all hot and sticky. I was a mess."

"What! You can move your ears," squealed Plumpkin in delight. "You can actually make your ears move? You can make them go where you want them to go?"

"Yes," replied Annie, taken by surprise. "Don't you want to hear the rest of my story?"

"Oh sure, but to be able to move your ears is just amazing. I would love to be able to move mine. They just fall down across my eyes so that I can't see very well. To be able to move them would be magic. Carry on, I'm all ears," Plumpkin said with a snigger.

"Well," Annie continued, feeling braver now that she was talking to Plumpkin. "As I stood there shaking, I suddenly realised that it was all in my head. None of the other horses were worried by you. Yes, they were curious, and we all played along with your game at the gate, because we like our games, too. But I realised I was scaring myself. You hadn't done anything to hurt me, and the only thing I was reacting to was the fear of being frightened. You made me aware that when I came to the fence to look for you, instead of looking to make sure you were still there and hadn't escaped in order to eat me, that I could just look for you and see what you were doing. And by doing that one small thing, it made me feel different about you and myself. Suddenly, every day, I began to like you and myself a little more and I wasn't so scared of being left alone in the field when the others moved away. In fact, I even began to look forward to my daily visit to the fence, just so I could see you. I even found myself smiling and laughing as I watched you being naughty, chasing the dogs or running around the garden. So you see, you helped me to overcome my fears by being you. You taught me that the best way was to look at my fears differently. I knew you wouldn't be going away, so I had to learn to change myself, to change the pictures in my head, and it worked."

"But, I still don't fully understand how I've helped," said Plumpkin with a frown upon her face. "I'm just a pig in a field."

"Exactly," replied Annie with a smile. "You continued to be you. Being naughty, being dirty, and even smelly, too. You were just you. Every day you went about your business unaware of my problem because they were my fears and worries, not yours. I had to learn that you weren't going to eat me. You made me face my fears and worries, as none of the other horses and ponies were frightened of you, only me. So every day, by standing and looking at you, I learned to feel better about myself, by not being so afraid of you. So you see, you did teach me. By being what you are, you taught me how to be strong and face my fears. The more I came to the fence and looked for you, the less afraid I became and the better I felt about myself as my confidence grew. So here I am today, to say thank you."

"Well, in that case, you can do something for me in return," Plumpkin said with a twinkle in her little eyes, lost beneath her huge ears.

"Anything," said Annie, unsure as to what was coming next.

"Scratch my back," laughed Plumpkin, knowing that perhaps Annie wasn't that brave yet.

"I'm not so sure about that one. It's not that I'm scared of you. You just smell a little odd. I think I may just have to live in the field for a couple of days so that I can get used to the smell of your mud," replied Annie, not quite sure about what she should do next. To walk away now would be rude; maybe someone would come to her aid and rescue her from this embarrassment.

Fortunately, Plumpkin came to her aid; she was, after all, a very kind and caring pig. "I'll let you off this time, but there's always tomorrow. Anyway, it's time for tea. See you later, alligator," she shouted as she ran toward her home.

"Alligator, where?" shouted Annie a little worried at the thought of something else to worry about. Actually, Annie didn't even know what an alligator was.

"It's a saying the human uses, it rhymes with later. Don't worry, Annie," Plumpkin shouted back, already her mind was somewhere else.

"No, I won't. It must be time for my tea, too. See you later, alligator," Annie shouted back, although Plumpkin was long gone. In the distance, she could see Plumpkin's nose was already in the trough enjoying her food.

The Circus Came to Town

❧⊱⊰❧

It was another cold and wet day and everyone on the farm was
fed up, bored, and had nothing to do. They were fed up eating
the hay and the fields were too wet and muddy to play in. They
needed something to do.

"I know," Monty called out, "we could play hide and seek."

"We played that one yesterday," Tilly replied, even she
was fed up. "We need something new to do, we need to stretch
ourselves."

"What do you mean?" Misty asked. He was always stretching
himself, usually it was by yawning and stretching his neck out to
see what he could find to eat.

"I know," Tsar spoke from the back of the herd, "we could
have a competition."

"A what?" Big Jed spluttered; he'd never heard of such a
thing.

"A competition," Tsar replied. "A little birdie told me that
the circus has come to town, in fact, it's parked a few fields
away, so perhaps we could offer ourselves and join the circus."

"I've never heard anything so funny in my life," Annie
snorted. She sounded a little like Plumpkin, the pig. Perhaps
she'd been spending too much time with her newfound friend.

"Oh, I think it's a wonderful idea," little Hettie piped up,
turning her head so that she could swish her beautiful, long, blonde

37

mane. Of course she was showing off, Hettie just loved doing that, but she was a very beautiful little pony and she knew it.

"Okay, okay, I get the picture. We're all fed up and want something to do, but join the circus? We're not exactly what you would call circus horses. Look at us, we're all dirty, with mud up to our elbows. Who'd look at us?" Jed asked. He had an air of authority about him. "Okay, to make you all happy and to give us something to do, we'll have a competition."

"Oh goody," Hettie squealed as she ran out of the barn. "I'm going to tell everyone on the farm; it's going to be such fun. Can I go first?"

"Hang on a minute," Jed shouted after her, "we haven't decided what the competition is for. Oh well, never mind, let's just see what everyone can do. We'll call it, 'show us what you're good at.'"

"That's brilliant," Misty laughed. "I'll win that easily because I can do lots of things."

"Now wait a minute, it has to be a fair competition, otherwise there's no point to it," Annie spoke out in defence of the little ones. "Anyway, Hettie has gone off to tell everyone on the farm; therefore, it's not just us horses who are going to perform and by the way, we need some judges to make it fair."

"Who can we get? We need someone who doesn't live with us." Rosie spoke for the first time, scratching her head, as she thought about who would be a good and fair judge. "I've got it, we could ask Eddie, the owl, Jackie, the jackdaw, and Colin, the crow, they're regular visitors here, but they don't actual live with us."

"Great idea, send for them, and let's get this show on the road," Jed suggested, as he was about to go out of the door. "Oh and how about Sammy, the squirrel, too, that way he won't want to show us how good he is at getting into things."

And so it was, that on that cold and rainy day, all the animals down on the farm suddenly found that they had something to do and think about. They all went off in different directions, to decide what they were good at, and what their act would be. It was agreed that they would have a day to rehearse and so the show would be in two days' time.

The day quickly arrived and everyone was in high spirits, or was it nerves? It was hard to tell, but the atmosphere was electric, and everyone looked much happier than they had been for days. It didn't even seem to bother them that it was still raining. The big barn was the chosen venue, and as she had requested, Hettie was the first to appear. Everyone lined up around the sides of the barn and for today only, the pigs were allowed to be there, too. Usually pigs and horses don't get together, so this was a very special day for everyone.

Hettie swished her beautiful, long, blonde mane by moving her head and neck from side to side and she danced and circled to the applause and cheers from the audience watching. Colin, the crow, signalled that her time was up and that it was time for the next act. Misty was next and he'd decided that he was going to show off his talent for counting. He used his front legs to count with and asked for numbers to be shouted out so that he could add them together. He could even do subtraction and finished his performance with a bow, in the direction of the judges, of course, hoping to gain a few extra points.

Next up was Monty and Tsar; they showed off their skills by playing together. They ran around the barn to the whoops and cheers of everyone and ended their display with Tsar lying down and Monty standing on him, pretending to be the winner.

The cats had decided on this special occasion that they would join forces and do an act together. They impressed everybody by climbing up the walls of the barn and then flying through the air narrowly missing the heads of everyone there, except for the judges, who were way up high in the rafters of the barn so that they could get a better view. The acts continued, each one doing their own thing, and all receiving rapturous applause with encouragement and praise.

The last act on was Plumpkin and Penelope and everyone wondered what on earth they were going to do. Surely they weren't going to stand there and eat, or were they going to dig a hole, because these were the only things that the animals thought pigs were good at. To everyone's surprise, Plumpkin and Penelope had decided that they should end the show with something truly spectacular. A large ramp was brought into the barn which they proceeded to run up at great speed and taking off, they appeared to fly effortlessly through the air and landed some distance away.

It was agreed by everyone there that they were the winners, because no one could believe their eyes. Who ever thought they'd live to see two pigs flying? But in fact, they were all winners because it took everyone taking part to make the day, no matter how big or small they were, they were all important and a good day was had by all.

Everyone learned a most important lesson that day, and that was that they could all get along and work together when given a reason to do so. Even the cats, who were normally so fiercely independent, found that they could quite happily play together. Everyone agreed that they'd all had a great time. Not only did they surprise themselves by what they achieved, but they were also surprised by what their friends could do, too. They even thought it would be a really good idea to do it again. They also learned that it's a state of mind as to how they felt, and that they could choose to be happy or sad, fed up, or keen and eager to try something new. Every one of them walked away feeling much better about themselves, and because they'd been encouraged by their friends, their confidence levels had risen, too, so much so, that they all wanted to do it again.

It Wasn't Easy

Well, guess what, it was another rainy day and all the horses were standing inside the barn for some relief from the drops of rain that keep falling.

"I'm fed up with this weather," Tsar spoke first, although of course, they were all as equally fed up, because they couldn't go out and enjoy what they loved doing most, eating the green grass. It was lost somewhere beneath the muddy water that was lying on top of it. "I know, let's have another competition, we could pretend that we're auditioning for the circus, it's still in town you know," he offered as a way of getting their approval.

It seemed to me that it was Tsar who was trying to persuade everyone to join in. He's a lovely pony, but the biggest problem he has is that he finds it very hard to keep his focus on any one thing for too long, because he's so easily distracted. I know that feeling, because I can be easily distracted, too, especially when it comes to chasing squirrels.

I suppose Tsar needed a new challenge to stop him from thinking he was bored. The only problem when someone keeps saying they're bored and yawns a lot, is that everyone around them begins to yawn, too. He was making me feel quite sleepy, and just as I was beginning to feel my eyelids closing everyone started moving around, shuffling into position, so that they could all see the big black horse, Jed, who was about to speak.

"Attention everyone," Jed boomed with his usual voice of authority. "Because we all enjoyed the performances everyone

42

gave the other day, and we all learned something new just by watching them, how about we all take turns to teach everyone else what we do best. Is that a good plan or not?" He hesitated, waited a moment while everyone thought about it, and then continued. "I think it's a really good idea. It will give us all an opportunity to learn how to do something new, which will get us thinking, instead of just standing here feeling fed up and bored. What about it?"

"I think it's a brilliant idea and everyone should take part, no one should be left out, because that way it will teach us to help one another, too. It'll be fun and a challenge to rise up to. I'm definitely for it," Rosie responded, with a giggle and a little excitement in her voice.

"Me too," Annie piped in.

"Me too," little Hettie was next, followed by everyone else; and so it was agreed by all. They would all attend the class, and because they had been so impressed by Misty's counting skills, they thought he should go first.

Now, you're probably wondering where the pigs were for this first lesson. Well, I have to tell you that Penelope and Plumpkin were fast asleep. You see, pigs just adore mud, and the rain had made the earth so soft and muddy that they just couldn't resist digging extra big holes, and they'd worn themselves out.

Now, I wasn't too sure about staying, because, to be honest, being as superior as I am, I didn't think I needed lessons. But then I decided it might be fun to watch the horses, just to find out how Misty was going to teach them all how to count.

There was an air of excitement, a buzz you might say, and it wasn't coming from the bees. As I watched, everyone got themselves into a comfortable position ready to watch Misty, who stood in the middle of the barn so that everyone could see him. Clearing his throat he began. "Welcome to our first lesson and thanks for choosing me." He shuffled from one hoof to another, looking quite uncomfortable as everyone looked at him. He stood in silence for a few moments, and then spoke again. "I'm not so sure, now that I'm standing here, that I know how to teach you what the human taught me. I don't know where to begin. I'm so sorry," he said as he began to walk away.

"But you were so clever the other day, you added up and took away," Tsar spoke with a sigh. "I'm so disappointed. I wanted to learn something new today. I've even been training my mind to stay focused. I've been training in secret, as I wanted to impress you all. I know you all think I'm just being naughty and seeking attention, but I'm not really. I find it really difficult to keep my attention focused on one thing, because too many other things come into my mind and then I don't know which way to go. After the competition, 'to find out what you were good at,' I decided that I needed to do something, so I gave myself some exercises to do. At first it was a little hard, because other thoughts kept flying in, like the bats that fly around the barn at night, they're so quick, you see them and then they're gone. These flying thoughts, I decided, were just minor irritations and had to go.

"Little by little, I worked it out that the less attention I gave them, the slower they got, and the slower they got, the more I could manage them, and the more I could control them, the easier it was for me to decide which ones to keep and which to let go of. It didn't take me long to realise that the less I had going on in my head, the easier it was to keep my concentration and focus on one thing at a time. So, I'm sorry if I sound disappointed, but this was going to be my chance at showing off my new skills to impress you all."

"It's okay, Tsar, we understand," Rosie said, as she walked over to him and gave him a reassuring kiss on the nose. "It took a lot of courage to say all of that, and you've certainly impressed me with your honesty." Then turning toward Misty she said, "I think it's very brave of you, too, Misty, to admit that you can't teach what you know how to do so well. To *know* is one thing, to *teach* is another, for it takes patience and understanding to be a good teacher, and to be honest, Misty, you don't have much in the way of either of those qualities," Rosie tilted her head slightly as she looked at Misty with such love and respect, that he couldn't be angry with her, even if he'd tried.

"I know, Rosie, and thank you for your honesty," Misty replied, holding back the rawness of the emotion and the embarrassment he felt, too. "Today has been a very important day for me to learn humility, because I admit I was arrogant, thinking I was much better than all of you. But standing here alone, and admitting my inability to teach you all how to count has taught me an important lesson. It's not about what we think we can do, but what we *can* do that counts in life. Also, it's made me realise how important you all are to me as my friends, which is why you all made it easier for me to admit to you what I cannot do."

Suddenly, there was a loud cheer, as everyone in the barn applauded Misty for his honesty. In everyone's eyes, their respect for him had grown, and they all moved in closer around him as if to give him a hug, not that he needed it, of course, but just to show him that their support was there.

"I know, I know," Rosie shouted out excitedly, in order to be heard. "Why don't we ask Eddie, the owl, to fly in and give us some lessons on counting? He's very wise and I'm sure he'll know how to teach us. I'm sure we'd all like that, especially Tsar, that way he'll have his chance to show off his new skills and impress us all."

"Rosie, you're always so good at finding solutions and making suggestions. I think that would be a brilliant idea," Misty replied with a tear in his eye, very thankful to Rosie for having just taken all the pressure off him.

"Time to send for Eddie, the owl," Jed called out. "Send Mr. Robin Redbreast, the messenger, he'll find him. Tell him to come as quick as he can, we don't want to lose the opportunity of the day when everyone is so eager to learn something new, do we?"

Well, would you have believed it, horses and ponies eager to learn something new? There's always something happening down on the farm. Now I can look forward to watching how Eddie the owl teaches them some new tricks. I'm sure it'll be fun to watch.

It's all been too exciting today for a little cat like me. The sun has just come out, so I'm off now to find some soft, sweet smelling hay on which to make a bed, then I'll close my eyes and dream of counting squirrels.

Eddie, the Wise Owl

Mr. Robin Redbreast made his way to the big oak tree where he knew Eddie, the owl, lived. Tapping on the outside of the trunk, next to a rather large hole, he could hear muffled sounds coming from within.

"Who's out there disturbing my peace?" Eddie shouted. "Can't an owl get some sleep nowadays? You'd better have a good reason; otherwise, you're for the high jump."

"Sorry to disturb your sleep," Mr. Robin Redbreast stuttered. "I have an urgent request from Big Jed."

"Big Jed? Who's Big Jed?" Eddie inquired. "And what does he want with me?"

"He's the big black horse that lives in the barn with all the other horses and ponies," Mr. Robin Redbreast, replied, trying very hard to remain calm. "I'm not sure why he needs you, but I know it's urgent; something to do with teaching the animals on the farm how to count."

"Count? Animals count? Never heard of such a thing, but then, what do I know?" Eddie spoke directly at poor Mr. Robin Redbreast, who didn't quite know where to put himself; after all, he was only the messenger. "All right, I'll go and help them out; I didn't want to sleep anyway. I had a bad night's hunting last night, so I need something to take my mind off my empty tummy."

Eddie was a very wise owl and knew that he would need

some help if he was going to teach the horses how to count. He already had a picture in his head of what he was going to do, but he would need some assistance, if his plan was going to work. It was important that his assistant had fingers, so that they could pick up sticks.

"Would you be able to find Sammy, the squirrel, and give him a message?" Eddie asked Mr. Robin Redbreast.

"Certainly," Mr. Robin Redbreast replied, "anything to help."

"Would you kindly tell him it's urgent and to come to the barn where the big horses live as soon as he can?"

"I'm on my way, see you there," he said, as he took off. On looking back over his shoulder, he could already see Eddie, the owl, in flight.

"Well, I'm not sure if I can teach the animals on the farm how to count, and I don't know why they need to do it anyway," Eddie said out loud, as he flew through the air on his way to the barn to meet the horses. "They say that you learn something new every day. I guess today could be my lucky day in solving one of life's mysteries—finding out why horses want to count."

It didn't take Eddie long to reach the barn where all the animals were waiting, as Big Jed wouldn't let them leave. He kept telling everyone that the day was too important and that no one should leave feeling disappointed. There was a big sigh of relief from Big Jed when he saw Eddie come flying in through the big open doorway.

Eddie landed on Jed's back and walked up his neck to whisper in his ear. "I have a plan and I'm just waiting for Sammy, the squirrel, to arrive. Can you get everyone in line, so that they can all see me? And I think that being a little small, it would be better if I stayed on your back."

"That's perfectly fine," Jed whispered back. He didn't want anyone to hear what they were saying. Getting everyone's attention by giving a loud cough, he spoke in his usual manner of authority, "Can you all line up please, and then we'll get started. Just in case you don't know him, this is Eddie, the wise owl, and he's come here today to teach us all how to count, at the request of Tsar and Misty Blue."

Both Tsar and Misty looked at one another and shook their heads; they hadn't really meant for any of this to happen. Tsar had just wanted to do something positive with the time they spent in the barn, instead of being bored and fed up. And Misty, having admitted that he couldn't teach his friends how to count the way the human had taught him, thought that by owning up, it would be the end of it. Now they were all standing here, waiting to be taught by an owl. Wow, this was going to be some lesson!

There was lots of noise going on in the barn, even though they were all talking in whispers, when suddenly everything went very quiet and silent, as Sammy, the squirrel, ran in and jumped up on Jed's back, to talk to Eddie.

"What do you want me to do?" he asked Eddie. The only thing he knew was that his tiny fingers were needed for some important work.

"I need you to find me five long sticks. I've got an idea in my head and I need you to make it work. Will you help us?" Eddie asked, hopeful that Sammy would know where to look.

"Of course, it would be my pleasure," Sammy spoke with pride in his voice; he'd never been asked to help anyone before. "I'll be back in a minute," and with that he was gone. He knew exactly where to look for the long sticks and true to his word, he was back in no time, dragging the sticks behind him.

"Good, we can get going now." Eddie shifted his position, as Jed walked into the middle of the barn where everyone could see Eddie.

"Right, the first thing we need to do is to count out the

numbers, so that you all know which number follows which number. Ready? One, two, three, four, five, six, seven, eight, nine, and ten." Everyone joined in, all shouting out the numbers at the same time, repeating them again and again, until everyone got the hang of it and they knew all the numbers off by heart. It sounded very loud and everyone seemed to be enjoying the whole process.

Eddie continued. "We won't go any further than ten. Okay. Now, I need you to go back to one and this time, we're going to add one to each number. Ready? One plus one makes two, two plus one makes three, three plus one makes four. Very good, you're all much better at this than I thought you would be. Five plus one makes six."

"Please Eddie," Tsar called out, "you've missed one out. We didn't do four plus one makes five."

"Didn't I? Oh well, never mind," Eddie spluttered, trying to keep his composure. "Tsar has put us right, so let's continue. Six plus one makes seven, seven plus one is eight, eight plus one is nine, and nine plus one is ten. Well done, everyone, now for the real test. Tsar, I wonder if you would be a really good chap and help."

"I'd be only too pleased to help," Tsar replied, puffing his chest out with pride. "I was hoping you'd ask me to do something. I'm so excited," he said as he fidgeted, moving from one hoof to the other, looking a little nervous now at suddenly finding himself becoming the centre of attention.

"Right Tsar," Eddie began, "can you add two and two together?"

"I can, it makes four," Tsar replied. He felt so pleased with himself for having been able to find the right answer. It wasn't as hard as he thought it was going to be.

"Well done," Eddie congratulated Tsar on his correct answer.

"Can you tell everyone how you arrived at the answer?"

"Certainly," Tsar replied, feeling even more pleased with himself. "I looked down at my front feet and counted two and then I added my back feet, which I knew I had two of as well, and then in my head, I went through the numbers and made it four."

"Excellent. Sammy, if you please, would you lay the sticks out on the ground, so that everyone can see them," Eddie continued, looking around his audience, to see that everyone was looking directly at him, sitting on Jed's back. Meanwhile, Sammy positioned the sticks, laying them out very neatly, as he, too, counted in his head, one, two, three, four, and five.

"Sammy," Eddie spoke directly to him, "I want you to take two sticks away and then I want everyone to tell me how many are left."

"Three," everyone shouted, followed by a loud cheer.

"And take away one more," Eddie requested. "What does that leave?"

"Two," everyone shouted again, all feeling very pleased with themselves. Who'd of thought it, animals counting?

"Right, now for an even harder test; has anyone ever heard of Roman numerals?" Eddie asked to a stunned audience. Not a murmur came from anyone's lips, just silence.

"Well, I guess from that response, you don't know what they are, in which case, this is definitely going to be something new for you to learn today. The Romans didn't use numbers like we use today, they used sticks instead as a way of counting and writing, so one stick represents?" he waited for a response from the crowd. "Come on, it's easy."

"One," Tsar shouted out.

"And if Sammy puts two sticks down on the ground?"

"Two," Tsar called out again. "We're making this hard, aren't we, because you've given it a different name?"

"Yes, is the simple answer; it isn't hard, in fact, it's very easy, all you have to do is think about it. Everything is still the same, one plus one makes two, etc. etc.; the only difference is that it looks different, because we're using sticks. I could have used the sticks before and it wouldn't have been a problem. I could have used carrots, but you would have eaten them. The only thing I've done that is really different is that I've given them a name, that's the only thing that's changed. So if Sammy adds another stick, how many does that make?" Eddie asked, in the hope that they would all begin to understand the process of counting sticks, instead of just saying numbers.

"Three," Tsar calls out again. "I can do this; ask me another please, Eddie."

"Okay," Eddie responded. "You're doing really well, Tsar. What if we add another two sticks? How many does that make?"

Now this wasn't so easy, because Tsar knew he had four legs, so four was an easy number to get, but now there was an extra leg and if he could just remember the table they'd said earlier, four plus one made five. "Five," he shouted out.

"Well done. Now I'm going to confuse you even more, because the Romans were very clever, they knew they couldn't keep on adding sticks. Creating long lines of sticks would mean nothing, so they came up with an idea of shortening the numbers. Using less sticks, meant more in numerical terms. Is everyone still with me?" Eddie asked, looking around for those nods of agreement, rather than the nods that meant they'd all gone to sleep. He was so enjoying this, he never got asked to teach much nowadays.

"Good, you're all still with me. So instead of five sticks, they decided that the letter V would be a substitute for the five sticks in a line. Sammy, would you be so kind as to make a letter

V with two sticks; so from now on, V means five. Have you all got that?"

Again they all nodded, they were all concentrating as hard as they could on what Eddie was saying, and their little brains were whirling into action trying to remember everything he'd said, as well as having to look at the sticks on the ground. Just as well Eddie had chosen sticks, because carrots being sort of the same shape, but much tastier wouldn't have lasted very long, there would have been a stampede to see who could get to them first.

"Now, Sammy is going to place one stick in front of the V. When it goes in front, it needs to be taken away from the number and when it goes after it, then it is added to the number, so what number are we talking about when we see the letter V?" Eddie asked to make sure everyone was still with him and understood the principle.

"Five," Hettie called out, she wanted to show everyone that ponies were just as bright as horses, cats, and dogs.

"Well done. And do you know the answer to five minus one?" he asked.

"Four, and by adding one, it makes six," Hettie replied, feeling very proud of herself; she found counting sticks quite interesting, not that she'd done it before.

"I'm very impressed by you all. Do you think you've done enough for the day or do you want to continue?" Eddie asked, hoping that they'd enjoyed his lesson so far.

"Talking on behalf of everyone," Misty stepped forward, so that he could continue, "I would like to thank you for a most interesting lesson. I know I have found it to be most helpful, but I think we should end here, as we all need time to digest what you've taught us. Thank you for your time and effort."

"It's been my pleasure and I've enjoyed doing it," Eddie responded. "And may I say, I thought you all did exceptionally well, far better than I thought you'd do. Call on me again when you want to learn something else," and with that he flew off Jed's back and out of the doorway, followed by Sammy, the squirrel, who thought it was best to leave now, in case the cats decided that their next lesson was to see who could chase him up the nearest tree. One by one the others left, too, as they each went off to find their own space, where they could stand quietly and process all they'd learned that day.

Monty

"Good morning everyone, what a lovely morning it is," I say that to them every morning because it gets the day off to a better start. I don't usually get many answers; the horses don't like getting up too early, but the chickens can't wait to get out of their house. They usually fly out and if I'm not careful, they can bowl me right over, as when they're in flight, nothing stops them. I nearly gave Eric, the cockerel, and myself a big shock this morning. I was so eager to do my usual morning round of seeing who was up and who was still asleep, running from place to place at full speed, that we both came round the corner at the same time, from different directions of course, and being the agile cat that I am, I saved the day. It also saved Eric's feathers and my fur from flying all over the place, too, as he's a very big cockerel, so my little body would have been quite bruised.

Cats are well-known for their quick thinking, well, to be honest we have to be, otherwise we'd be getting into an awful lot of trouble. I'm sure we do so many daredevil stunts because we think we can and it's only when we're doing them that we usually find we can't. I don't think we do much forward planning; it's more a spur of the moment thing, which has lately gotten me to thinking. That's another one of my jobs; I'm a very observant cat. I spend a lot of my time watching and waiting and thinking.

55

I also have very good ears and eyes to listen and observe with. Oh yes, we animals have to learn to listen with both sets of eyes and ears because every part of the body talks. Did you know that? Well, it's true. When you're happy and excited, your voice gets louder and higher; you'll also be more animated, which means your body will move more, especially your hands and sometimes your feet. You'll be smiling and your eyes will be sparkling. When you're sad, your voice will be softer and lower, your head will be lower, and your whole body will be rounder, so you see, you don't just talk with your mouth, every part of you has something to say and it's just the same with us animals. It is called body language. So, I thought that today I would like to go and check in on the ponies, because those horses are a bit too big for my little paws. You know I'm very naughty at times because I run between their legs, but then I'm so fast, that I've gone before they even know I'm there. Well, I like to think that they wouldn't really tread on a little fella like me.

"Hi guys, I was wondering if you could help me today, I'm looking for some answers to a very serious question."

"Oh no, not you again, don't you ever stop thinking?" Tiger replied, turning away from me. He'd given me his answer loud and clear.

"Don't worry about Tiger, it's a little too early for him," Hettie replied. "What can we do to help you?"

"Well, I was wondering if you ponies are as confident as us cats," I asked with the sort of look on my face that said, 'please help me.'

"Hmmmm," Hettie sighed. "That's not an easy one to answer, but I'll give it a go."

"Thanks Hettie, I'm all eyes and ears," I replied, getting myself into a comfortable position.

"You see," Hettie began, "it all depends upon the person.

Each of us is different and better at doing different things. Take you for instance, you climb trees all day long, so you don't even think about how you do it anymore, you just do it. Us ponies couldn't even begin to think about climbing trees because we're not made to climb them, so it would never even enter our heads; on the other hand, you wouldn't be happy standing in a field all day long eating grass, would you?"

"No, that's boring," I replied. As I changed position, I thought this conversation was going to get a little more interesting.

"Exactly my point," Hettie smiled, knowing that cats, dogs, and horses are all so different, that this question was going to be difficult to answer in a short sentence. "Because we are all so different, confidence comes in many forms. Take my boy, Monty, now there's a confident little fellow, nothing bothers him, he never sees danger on the other side of the fence. In fact, he climbs through so many fences, that I constantly worry about him. You see, because he doesn't see the danger, he never stops to think about what he's doing. I do, because that's my role as his mummy. I have to let him have a certain amount of freedom to explore, because that way he finds out what he can and cannot do, but there comes a point when I have to be able to stop him before he gets hurt."

"I don't think about what I'm doing, should I?" I asked with a serious look on my face.

"Sometimes, when you're so confident at what you do, it can get you into trouble, because you don't stop to think about the consequences. Remember every action causes a reaction." Hettie spoke with such softness in her voice that it brought a tear to my eye. "Shall I tell you about the time my Monty overstepped the mark and got himself told off by everyone?"

"Yes please, go on," I urged her to continue. I love listening to stories, so I made myself more comfortable, curling up by

Hettie's hooves.

"Well," Hettie continued, "it was a cold, late winter afternoon and the human had come to give us our dinners. She was busy in the feed room preparing all the nice food for us to eat, when my dear son, Monty, decided that he would climb through the fence. It was his party trick; he thought it was funny, and he did it to impress the bigger horses because they could only get their heads through the fence. He also did it to tease them, too, because if the gate to the barn was open, he would go in and help himself to extra hay. Anyway, I digress. He'd got himself through the fence and we were all there watching him, whilst waiting for our buckets to appear. Buckets are very important to horses and ponies because they contain food. Well, we couldn't believe our eyes. He went up to the feed room door, and with his mouth, he pushed the bolt across. We were all shouting, 'No!' But it was too late; he locked the human in. He was now in big trouble. He was going to have to face us all, and he couldn't escape this one."

"What did you do?" I asked, all excited as to what was going to happen next.

"Nothing, we couldn't do anything. Monty was the only one who could climb through the fence and as much as we all pleaded with him to open the door, he couldn't. He couldn't work out how to pull the bolt back, it was easy to push it forward, but backwards was a different exercise and he hadn't learned to do that one, yet. And the poor human, we could hear her shouting inside. It got colder and colder, darker and darker, and all our tummies were beginning to rumble. Oh boy, he was in big trouble, and the longer it went on, the worse it was getting. The big horses were getting very angry and I was beginning to feel very sorry for my little boy. I knew he hadn't meant to cause this much trouble, his problem had been that he hadn't thought about what he was doing and the effect it would have. Remember cause and effect, whatever you do on the one hand will have an effect on the other hand."

"Did it have a happy ending? Did the human manage to get out and feed you all?" I asked, hoping that it did.

"Yes," Hettie continued, "fortunately after a long time of trying various means of sliding the bolt back, we suddenly heard this almighty thud and the door burst open. She was not amused; in fact, she was so angry, that she got hold of my little boy by his mane and pulled him into the yard with the big horses."

"Did they tell him off, too?" I asked, feeling very sorry for my friend Monty. I'm sure he hadn't meant to cause so much trouble.

"No, by now we were all so hungry and relieved to see the human and our buckets, that they let him eat his dinner in peace," Hettie said with relief in her voice.

"Did you tell him off?" I asked, feeling sure Hettie wouldn't be too hard on her son.

"In a way, I did. I reminded him that it is one thing to be confident and to know that you are good at doing some things well, but it is completely different to be so confident that you don't stop to think about what you're doing and how you can hurt others by your actions."

"Was he sorry?" I asked.

"Yes, he was," Hettie continued. "After we had all finished eating our dinner, he went around to everyone and apologised and promised that he would never lock the human in again, but he couldn't promise not to climb through the fence again."

"What did they do? He was very brave to do that, wasn't he?" I asked, thinking to myself that maybe the next time I went to play a trick on someone I'd better make sure my plan would be safe and wouldn't hurt anyone.

"It was the least he could do in the circumstances; after all, he'd caused us all some discomfort and embarrassed me, his dad, and his sister. So yes, he did have to go and apologise for his actions, otherwise he'd not think twice about doing it again, would he?" Hettie huffed, finishing her sentence with a stamp of her hoof.

"No, you're absolutely right. I know you've made me think. I never thought about being too confident or the effects it might have on others, but I see what you're saying. The next time I attempt to climb the biggest tree, I'll make sure that I can climb it and not find out halfway up that it's too big and I'm stuck and I have to shout for help." I looked Hettie right in the eye, so that she could see I was telling the truth, and I meant it.

"Exactly. Caution is like a little warning light that says you need more lessons and to be better prepared. Every one of us can do something. Some things we're very good at, whilst there are other things that we need a little more practise at doing, and there are some things that we haven't even tried, so we don't know if we can do them or not."

"Oh, I get it," I replied. "It's not that we're not confident, we just don't know how good we are, until we practice the next move."

"Exactly," Hettie replied all excited. "You have to try something new first, before you know how good you're going to be at doing it. Another important thing to remember is that you can't be good at everything. Everyone has something they're good at; you just have to keep trying until you find it."

"Thanks, Hettie. I think I need to go and lie down now. I need to sleep on everything you've said so that I'll remember it all. See you tomorrow. Bye," and with that I leapt to my feet and ran out of Hettie's stable to go and find a nice hay bale so that I could curl up, close my eyes, and go to sleep to dream about climbing the biggest tree I could find. Only, I never got to climb the tree, because I remembered what Hettie had said. There's no point trying to do something you're not prepared for, because it only leads to disappointment and tears; so instead, I dreamt about playing hide and seek with the chickens, as I like making Eric, the cockerel, jump, by surprising him, laying in wait until I can leap out and scare him. It is only a game and we both enjoy playing it.

What Dreams Are Made Of

I wonder if you believe in magic. I do. Shall I tell you why? Well, it's because every day I look around the world I live in and see the magic that's there. Not pretend magic, but real magic, like how the trees know when to come back to life in the springtime. How do the birds know when to build their nests? How does the chicken know when to go bed, and why do squirrels get up to such mischief? Do you ever stop for a moment and look around your world? If you did, you'd be amazed at what is out there for you to find.

Take for instance, the day that I went on a search, not that I was searching for anything in particular, I just took it into my head to go down into one of the other fields, the one that is supposed to be a bit special. I don't know exactly how or why, it's just special. If you'd asked me about it before, I'd have told you it was just an ordinary field; I'd checked it out many times before and found nothing out of the ordinary there, only on this particular day, everything in my world changed. I've already told you ages ago that I am a very special, magical cat, well, that's because I can create pictures, images in the human's mind to tell her that I want something. It always works; well, I guess it does, as she responds to my messages and that's why I say I have magical powers. Well, you would, wouldn't you?

So going back to my wanderings, no, not my ramblings, my wanderings around the estate. Checking up on things as I do sort of helps the human out, although she isn't always aware of the patrolling job that I do, in fact, all of us cats do it, and it's something we like to do. We like to keep a check on who comes into our space, our territory, and whether they have our permission or not. We always have to be on the lookout for any stray cats that just might wander in to see what food is on offer. The human is well trained in feeding us and leaves plenty of food around to eat, just in case we get hungry.

For a change the sun was shining, so everywhere looked nice and bright. The different greens of the trees and grasses all seemed more vibrant, colourful, and brighter than usual, I guess that's why I did a double take, because it looked different somehow, yet I couldn't quite place my paw on it. I'm sure you get the picture. Sometimes you just can't find the right words to express what you're feeling and so it was on this particular day, that not only was the field odd and different, but it made me feel different, too, in a nice sort of way, alert yet calm, with a pleasant tingle, as if I had been given an unexpected present to open. Anyway, I stayed there out of curiosity as we cats are very curious creatures, and we just love investigating new things. I decided to explore the whole field and find out what had caused the change in it, although of course, on the surface all looked normal.

Sometimes, it's what we think we don't see that makes the difference. Do you know that your eyes register everything? They miss nothing, not even a tiny sparkle or glint in the grass. They'll see and register it all. It doesn't matter that you don't remember everything, because there is another part of you that does. A bit like a computer, where you store things in files, so that when you want them, you can open them and look inside. Well, you work in much the same way, only sometimes what happens is that the brain doesn't always register the information, because it doesn't know what it is. If it has no picture to compare it to, then it may think it is rubbish and discard it. Can you imagine how much information your brain has to register each day, an enormous amount. Do you know you're better than any computer that has ever been built? The difference is that the computer has been programmed to recognise certain pieces of information, and you're still learning, so imagine what you're capable of. It's truly amazing when you stop to think about it. Just imagine what you could be capable of, if you put your mind to it.

Talking of minds, I was telling you about my experience in this little field that's long, narrow, and special. I'd climbed the fence and walked across the little wooden bridge when I had to stop and blink, because I thought I'd just seen a small human with wings fly past my face. I shook my head just to make sure my brain was still there. Yep, I could hear it moving around. I couldn't believe my eyes, was what I'd just seen real or imaginary? Are there such things as fairies? I know lots of people say they've seen them, and I know lots of horses that say they've seen big dragons in the hedgerows; of course, they're only kidding. It's just their reaction to the little sparrow that flies out of the hedge, only because they make such a song and dance about it, they have to create a huge dragon to make it worthwhile.

So do fairies, pixies, elves, and other tiny creatures really exist? Lots of stories have been written about them, so they could be real, couldn't they? In which case, one had just flown past me, so I needed to follow it and find out where it went to.

With my nose in the air, my ears pricked up, and my eyes wide open, I began to walk further into the field, all the while though, something kept catching my eye right over in the corner by the big oak tree. Slowly, I made my way to the big tree, looking and listening all the time. Now, do we create our imagination or are our imaginations already there, and we just add to them as we continue to learn and grow? This was a curious question for me to ask myself, because right then, I wasn't sure what was real and what was make-believe, but then, don't we have to make-believe it first, in order to make it real? You have to think about that one a little bit, don't you? Quite right, you do, I hear you say. You see, or maybe you don't, but the thought has to come first before the action, otherwise we wouldn't have movement. I couldn't climb the tree if I didn't think first that I wanted to be at the top, because otherwise my muscles wouldn't move me in the right direction. Our thoughts are sometimes our engines, because they move us. Imagine how powerful your thoughts are and what you can achieve by having them and using them, but of course, you have to be able to think in the right direction first, in order to go there. I know you're already on your way there right now.

Because I already felt odd, did my imagination take over, or did I really see something? Now you might say that it really doesn't matter, and I'd agree with you, because it's all down to belief. If you believe in something, then it becomes real to you and that's what counts. In the same way that when you believe in yourself and what you're capable of, you suddenly find that whatever you put your mind to, you can do it and succeed in ways that you never dreamt of. It all comes down to that mind over matter bit, so that what you thought at first was impossible, soon becomes possible, because you believe you can do it. There's nothing stopping you from practicing, taking small steps over and over again, in order to succeed at something, because, after all, practice makes perfect. Take me for instance, I have to keep practicing my balancing act, otherwise I'd fall off the fence and land up in the mud and that just wouldn't do for a special cat like me.

Well, getting back to my story, it turned out that my imagination that day was playing tricks on me, because the fairy turned out to be a little Firecrest, which is a very tiny bird with colourful stripes on its head. I'd never seen one before and because it was unfamiliar, I didn't have a picture to recognize it by; but, I do now, so the next time I see it, I'll be able to recognise it instantly. That's how our minds work; they build up large amounts of correct information that's stored for when we need to use it and when we do, it gives us access to knowledge and understanding. So the more you let your imagination out to play, the better you become at learning how to do new things. You begin to make the impossible possible, and by applying your knowledge and understanding to those new areas in your life, it makes you feel better, stronger, and more confident about yourself.

Do I still believe in fairies? Oh yes, because all the time I think there's something else out there in the world for me to find, something that I can't yet see, it makes me appreciate all that I can see and keeps my curiosity alive.

I'm off now; got to see what else I can find on my daily adventures. You just never know what other magic I might find. So, bye for now and we'll talk again soon.

Bo to the Rescue

There is a very special place called "Not Far Away, Very Close To Your Heart" where a number of fairies live and two in particular, one called Be True and the other called Never Lie.

Recently, in this land called Not Far Away, Very Close To Your Heart, a big giant had decided to settle down and build himself a big house with many rooms. This ordinarily wouldn't have been a problem, because the fairies that live in this special place are very accommodating and providing you are good and honest, everyone lives happily together, because they all know the rules; this means that all the time everyone is being good, the whole land is happy, and everyone wears a smile. As soon as one fairy does something that is considered bad or unfair, the sun stops shining and everyone wears a frown. That way everyone is responsible for keeping the sun shining and so it should have been that everyone lived happily ever after, but they couldn't, because of the big giant who wanted to move in and disturb their peace and happiness. They knew they couldn't stop him, because he was too big and they would never be able to control where he wanted to walk or even build his house. The biggest problem of all was that he could not see these tiny fairies that live in the land of Not Very Far Away, Very Close To Your Heart, because they only show themselves to very special people. They needed to do something, but what?

At first, they all talked about moving and rebuilding their homes somewhere else, but then they decided against it, because there would always be a big giant, wanting to move in to share their sunshine and happiness. It was agreed by all that they would have to do something to allow the fairies and the giant to live happily side by side. At this stage, however, they didn't exactly know what they could, or would be able to do, to achieve this. The fairies, Be True and Never Lie, thought that they'd like to help on this project and somehow managed to get elected onto the main committee. As it turned out, they were the only two members of the committee, as no one else joined; so, it was up to these two fairies to find the solution.

Sitting together trying to come up with something, Be True suddenly flapped her wings and shouted out excitedly, "We could go and meet him to explain our situation that we're very tiny and afraid of him because he could step on us and our homes without even realising that we're there. He would have to be very careful and watchful, but that way we could all live happily together."

"Brilliant idea, but there's just one problem," Never Lie offered. "If he can't see us, how will he hear us?"

"Good thinking, but I have a plan," Be True said as she started to fly away.

"Wait for me," Never Lie called out after her. "Where are we going?"

"Hurry up and you'll see. Come on, we've no time to lose." Be True flapped her wings even faster, she was on a mission as a great plan had suddenly popped into her head, and now she needed to find someone special who'd be able to help and put her plan into action.

Meanwhile, the big giant was having second thoughts about moving. His nickname was 'Not So Good,' because every time anyone asked him how he felt, he always replied, 'not so good.' Now everyone he met, instead of saying, 'good morning or good afternoon,' just said, 'hello, Not So Good' and walked away. Thinking that everyone felt sorry for him, the giant always nodded, which of course made him feel worse. He just couldn't break the habit, for try as he might, he always ended up saying, 'not so good' to any question he was asked. But now, he wasn't feeling so good over the move, what if it didn't work out, or he couldn't settle, or he didn't make new friends? He now had more worries than he'd ever had and was definitely living up to his name of Not So Good. What was he to do?

Once upon a sunny day, not so long ago, a blonde cat by the name of Bo Jangles had visited this very special place, called Not So Far Away, Very Close To Your Heart, without really knowing it. Whilst walking through this very special land, he'd caught a glimpse of a fairy or two as they'd fluttered by, but dismissed them because his eyes hadn't registered what he'd seen, which is what normally happens when we don't recognise something for the first time. Be True had been one of those fairies that had fluttered by that day, and now she was searching for him, because her plan involved Bo Jangles talking to the giant, Not So Good, and explaining their situation. The two fairies didn't have to fly for too long, before they came upon the blonde cat, lying along the branch of a big oak tree.

"You go first," Never Lie said to her friend, suddenly feeling very shy.

"Okay, but you stay close by, just in case," Be True said as she fluffed herself up, trying to make herself as big as she could, as she hovered very close to Bo's ear.

At first, Bo thought it was an irritating fly and took several swipes at it with his paw. Fortunately, Be True was very quick and moved out of the way. Never one to give up, she persisted. It took several attempts for her to get his attention, and in the end, she took to hovering right in front of his eyes, which unfortunately for Bo had the effect of making him go cross-eyed, but it worked. Suddenly, he could see this very tiny, beautiful, delicate fairy hovering right in front of him, frantically flapping her wings. In fact, it was the breeze he felt on his face that made him look ahead.

"Bo Jangles," Be True called his name out as loud as she could.

"You know my name?" Bo queried, trying to guess as to how she knew his name, but giving up after a nanosecond. This was unreal, yet at the same time something told him it was very real. He wasn't asleep, so he wasn't dreaming.

"Bo, we need your help," Be True began, "we have a big problem and you're the only one that can help us."

"Me? How?" Bo asked, totally taken aback by this wonderful request. He'd never been asked to help anyone before. This request made him feel very important and all fluffed up.

"Please help," Never Lie spoke this time.

"Another fairy? How many of you are there?" Bo asked.

"Lots of us, in fact, a whole village," Never Lie continued. "We live in a special place by the bridge."

"Oh, I know it, the field of magic where the sun always seems to shine," Bo replied, feeling very pleased with himself that he knew exactly where they lived. "I often go in there because it always feels so nice."

"We know you do, we often fly past you, and play games with you," Never Lie teased him. "That's the reason why the giant wants to live there. He thinks it will make him feel better. Do you think you can help us?" she asked, with a worried look on her tiny face and a tear just beginning to roll down her cheek.

"Of course I can and I will." Bo spoke with such confidence, that he even believed in himself, knowing that he'd find an answer to their problem. "Give me the details and I'll go and find him and explain everything to him."

Well, it turned out that the giant, Not So Good, was none other than the grumpy goat who lived next door. He had managed to find his way into the special field by pushing through a gap in the fence, under the bridge, where it had fallen down. Every time he went into the field, he felt so much better, so he thought that by living there it would cure him of his worries, and he could become a happy goat again.

Bo easily understood why the grumpy goat appeared to the fairies as a giant. They were so tiny that everything else around them looked so big. *I bet I must look like a lion in their eyes*, he thought to himself, with just the hint of a smile on his face.

Bo knew where to look for the giant, in the field next door, because he'd seen him on the odd occasion when he'd roamed a little farther than usual. He found him under a large oak tree scratching his back. As best as he could, he explained to Not So Good that it was his own state of mind that made him feel the way he did, that his friends and neighbours no longer stopped to speak to him because he was always so grumpy and miserable. He also explained that moving to the special field wouldn't really help him either, because the tiny fairies that lived there would be so frightened of him that they would leave. He explained that the fairies were really worried because Not So Good couldn't see them or their homes; he might step on them by accident or destroy their village. Bo made it clear to the goat that if the fairies left, they would take the sunshine and happiness away with them, and then poor, old grumpy Not So Good would be even grumpier.

"What do you suggest I do, Bo?" Not So Good asked, with his head bent low between his front feet. "I want to be happy, really I do, but everywhere I go, people just say my name and then walk away. I'm so lonely and I want to smile and laugh again."

"Do you really?" Bo asked with a twinkle in his eye. "Would you be willing to do anything to change?" he asked, as a plan began to grow in his mind. He could suddenly see the solution to everyone's problems.

"I'm going to ask the tiny fairies to come and sprinkle you with the magic fairy dust that they spread around the special field you so like going in to. But, they have to do it while you're sleeping. That way, it can work its magic and give you nice dreams to dream, so that when you wake up in the morning, the sun will be shining and you'll be happy. You'll feel so good that you'll make everyone feel good, too. You'll be smiling, so they'll smile back and soon everyone will be smiling. They'll be stopping to talk to you, because grumpy old Not So Good will be gone, he'll have gone away and in his place, a new person will have arrived, someone called, 'So Good.' How does that sound?" Bo asked with his paws crossed.

"That's a brilliant plan. I like it," said Not So Good as he picked his head up, Bo saw a sparkle in his eyes and the beginning of a smile that caused the corners of his mouth to curl upwards. "When can they sprinkle me with fairy dust?" he asked, eager to change his ways. He couldn't wait to be a happy, friendly goat again.

"Right now if you wish," Bo replied. "Close your eyes and just imagine you're in the special field of magic, where the sun is shining. You see two tiny fairies flying toward you. To you, they may look like dragonflies, but I can assure you, they're fairies carrying a pouch full of fairy dust. In the sunlight, you see it glistening, and as it begins to fall like gentle rain, your eyes begin to feel very heavy and tired and you fall into a deep sleep. When you're fast asleep with your eyes tightly closed, all your worries will be taken away from you. Happy dreams,"

Bo whispered into his ear and then, very gently and quietly walked away, leaving the fairies to do their work, while So Good enjoyed his sleep and his pleasant dreams, so that in the morning he would wake up all bright and happy.

"Thank you, Bo," Be True called after him, as she blew him a kiss that landed right on his little pink nose.

Bo felt so good with himself; he'd really enjoyed coming to the rescue and helping the tiny fairies that lived in the special field. Perhaps the next time he went into the field, they could all play together, now that they didn't have to move away.

Bo, the Explorer

Well, would you believe it? I woke up this morning and the sun was shining, it looked a glorious day, one that was going to be too good to miss. It was definitely a day for being outdoors, which meant it was the perfect day for an adventure. It would be nice to share it with someone so that we could have some fun together, but who?

I thought about asking little Monty because he likes adventures, but then I thought better of it. You see, Monty can't climb the trees or walk along the fences as his tiny hooves aren't like cat's claws that are made for clinging onto things, like curtains and furniture. My cousin, Lily, loves climbing up the curtains and then swings from them. The human isn't too pleased or impressed by her antics when she does this trick, but I have to say, she is so much fun to watch, it's as if she's on a race track, and sometimes she goes so fast that she falls off. Did I say fall off? No, that's definitely not right, cats never fall off anything, it may look like it, but we're really only pretending by making it look as if we're falling off.

Maybe I should ask Lily, at least then we could race one another. We could have a competition to see who could climb the tree the fastest, or see how far we could run along the fences without falling off. See, I've said it again. Of course I meant to say, without jumping off. As you know, our sense of balance is so remarkable, that we never fall off anything; we're just very good at pretending.

74

Cats are also very proud and would never admit to anything, just in case you thought it was the opposite, that way, we always get it right. I guess you could say we have lots of confidence. Confidence is that thing, that feeling that makes you do something. It's the thing that gets you started, because you believe that you can do it and then, when you start doing it, you find you can do it well. It makes you feel good about yourself because you're putting the right effort into it. It moves you forward and you feel even better about yourself than you did before, because you see and feel the result of that effort, and so on. As your confidence grows, your feelings about yourself grow too, it's simple.

So you see, each time I go exploring, I come back feeling really good about myself, and the things I've managed to do, even the little things mean something. Take the other day, it was just as sunny and everyone felt good, smiles all around. The horses and ponies were out enjoying the grass that was growing in their fields. The chickens were being really naughty, crossing the road without looking. A car had to slow right down; in fact, it had to stop, because they chose to walk across the road just as the car was coming round the corner. Do you know they walked across the road without a care in the world? It was as if they owned the road. That's chickens for you.

Me, now I know different. First I wait at the kerb, I listen, then I look both ways, and before I cross the road, I listen again, and I keep on listening as I run across it. Then I'm safely on the other side.

Where was I? Oh yes, now I remember, I was going to tell you about the other day when everyone was happy. Do you know that when the sun shines, and everyone smiles, it's because it makes us feel so good when we see its happy face and feel the warmth of it on our bodies, too.

So feeling good, I was doing my normal patrolling duties,

keeping a watchful eye on things, when I spotted something happening in the distance, down in the special field where the fairies live. Earlier I'd seen the human with the two dogs, Anna and Gem, taking a stroll across the field. Usually I'd join them, but today I decided to do my own thing. We cats quite like going for a walk, in fact, when the human is taking one of the ponies out for a walk, we like to join in. It must be quite a sight to behold, one human, one pony, two dogs, and four cats all walking in procession. Anyway, there I go again, skipping around what I was about to tell you.

Well, as you know, cats are curious creatures; we like to know what's happening on our patch. I guess you could say we're nosy. I always thought that was what my nose was for, sniffing out interesting things. I just couldn't resist it, I had to run down to the field and find out what was going on. Running as fast as I could, leaping into the air, I flew down there to find Gem and Anna playing. I'd never seen them play before, well, not like they were. They'd got hold of this large plastic pipe and I mean large, it was about seven metres in length and had an opening large enough for me to scramble into. Anna is a sniffer dog; she uses her nose to find things, like baby rabbits and mice and other animals, but not cats or chickens. Oh, that's gross, I hear you say, but it's life. We animals live to hunt or to be hunted, that's what happens. So, she was only doing what her instincts told her to do.

Do you know what instincts are? They're the feelings that make us do things, automatically, without having to think about them, or reason them out, like the pigeon who always finds his way home, or the baby that knows how to suckle its mother's milk. The way we know we must eat in order to stay alive or brush your teeth to keep them clean. Washing your hands when you've been to the bathroom, and you know how to cross the road safely.

All these things and many, many more you do automatically, because you do them instinctively. So Anna automatically knew there was something in that long plastic pipe, because her nose told her so, and she wanted to find out what it was. To do so, she had to ask Gem for help, because she needed Gem's strong jaws to bite through the plastic pipe. Dogs don't have knives or scissors like humans to cut through things. Between the two of them, Gem biting and Anna pulling, they eventually began to make the pipe smaller and smaller as they pulled it apart. It was so much fun watching them wearing themselves out, pulling and chewing, until Anna got what she wanted.

Dogs, I've decided, are very patient and determined when they set their mind on something. They follow it right through to the end and guess what? Because of that, they get their rewards. I'm not so sure about cats. I think we probably give up a little earlier and move onto something else that gets our attention. Do you stick at something until you've got the hang of it? You do, well done. Do you like trying out new things, too? You do, well done again. You have to keep trying new things because otherwise, you'll never know what you're good at. You mustn't stop trying just because it didn't work out the first time.

Like Anna and Gem, they had to keep working at making the large pipe smaller and smaller until it was so small, that Anna could reach what she was after. She'd smelt a nest of baby animals and wasn't going to give up until she got there. Only, when the nest fell out of the pipe, there weren't any little babies there. It was an old nest and they'd all grown up and moved away. Oh well, it was a good game. The dogs were exhausted, but they'd had such fun working together, each pulling and tugging at opposite ends, and when it wouldn't break, Gem used her teeth to bite through the plastic tube, because she knew that by doing so, it would help Anna to achieve her goal. Not that

I'm suggesting you try biting through a plastic tube. What I'm saying is that sometimes, when faced with a problem you want to solve, asking a friend to help is one way to solve it.

Now, where was I? Oh, I know. I was trying to work out who to invite on my day out exploring. Well, I think I may have had enough excitement for one day. Just telling you about how I watched the dogs working so hard and playing together has worn me out. I think it's time to find a nice soft place to lay my head down and sleep. I'll try again tomorrow, after all, who knows what tomorrow may bring, sunshine and smiles. Sweet dreams.

Annie Meets Sinbad

Well, would you believe it that Annie, now that she's got over her fears and worries, moves about from field to field all by herself. For many years she has always been someone's shadow. Some days it was Misty Blue or Rosie, other days it was Jed, as he would let her graze close by him so that she wasn't alone, but she would never be anywhere near Tsar, he wouldn't let her into his space. Perhaps it's not as odd as you think it sounds because animals, like humans, have their likes and dislikes. Some friends you'll like on Monday and by Friday, you don't even want to speak to them. At least you don't have to live with them, but family is different, you can't escape them, in much the same way that Annie couldn't really escape Tsar, as they live in the same field. In order to live happily together, they've had to learn to respect each other's space, by keeping a safe distance between themselves. This way they don't have to keep pulling faces at each other. Horses do that, you know, they've very good at pulling faces, as it tells the other horses to beware.

Now with horses, respect is a very big word in their vocabulary of body language. By showing respect, whether it's age related, size, or pecking order, it means that you cannot enter someone's personal space without their permission, and if you try to force your way in, beware. Horses don't generally fight one another; they pull faces and twitch their tails, a bit like us cats when we're onto something. Maybe it's our tail moving that gives us away.

Anyway, going back to my observations, horses are most interesting as every day is different to them. Every day they check one another out just to see who wears the crown of authority. It's usually the same order within the herd, but they check it out, anyway. I guess it gives them something to do.

We, cats, on the other hand are always doing something, going off somewhere to explore, sniffing out the opposition, patrolling the fields, always on the lookout for a small creature or two and if we're not doing any of the above, then you'll find us curled up in a ball, fast asleep until dinner time, and then we start all over again. I think you might say we have routines and rituals because we do the same things every day, and do you know, sometimes we have an order in which we do them. Do you have your own personal routine that you stick to? Does this routine or ritual have a purpose like us animals' have?

We just love our dinner ritual. We all come together at the same time and line up, waiting to be fed. I'm sure we do it sometimes just to annoy the human, as she gets so flustered with so many mouths to feed all at once, because even the dogs join in, too. Can you imagine it, six hungry mouths to feed and that's not counting the chickens waiting at the back door, or the horses that have already been fed.

I think that we're very clever in that we can remember to be somewhere at an allotted time, without even having a watch to look at. We can remember many other things, too, without even having to think about them. I think it could be called programming. Don't you think it's amazing that every morning you wake up, you know more than you did the day before, without really working at it? I do. What this means is that you can basically programme yourself to do anything. All you have to do is think about what you want to achieve and then take the first step toward achieving it.

Do you know that the first step is usually the hardest because we usually hesitate over taking it, wondering whether we have the confidence to go through with it or not? And that big one, what if it fails? Failure only occurs when we don't even try. So try you must, at whatever you decide to go for, and if you try, you'll always be successful, as success is measured by how you cope with handling the disappointment, if it didn't quite work out the way you expected it to.

Take for example the human, one day, well, for many days really, those pigs, Plumpkin and Penelope, had been leading the human in a merry dance; they kept escaping. No matter how much she tried to keep them in their enclosure, which wasn't small, they somehow managed to get out of it. The challenge the pigs had set themselves was to escape. The challenge to the human was how to keep them contained. Now, one was bound to succeed and the other to fail. So each day, a new challenge was offered.

One day, after many failed attempts, the human was determined she would win. What failure did for her was to teach her many new skills. She applied her mind to the workings of the pigs and how they managed to find so many new ways to escape. She learned new woodworking skills because she had to repair the fences or fill in holes, and eventually it all paid off, and the pigs were contained. Well, until they could devise a new plan of action. So on that occasion, their failure to succeed led them into having to think of new ways to escape; after all, they didn't want to leave the human without something to do. Each one gained from the experience and that's exactly what our daily lessons do for us, in the experience of life, they teach us something. They prepare us for the next lesson to come and so on, because no matter what, big or small, young or old, we never stop learning. Life always has something new to teach us, it's how we accept those lessons and what we learn from them that make a difference to our lives.

Now that Annie, who used to be so frightened of her own shadow that she used to jump if she saw it following her, thinking it was another horse, was wandering across the field all by herself. She was off to see the new arrivals at the bottom of the field, a flock of sheep that had come for a holiday. If she thought the pigs smelled, I wondered what she'd make of the sheep and their big, black, woolly bodies.

I couldn't help but watch as she approached the gate, for there standing on the other side of it was Sinbad, the ram. He was just as inquisitive about the big, brown horse approaching his field as she was in checking him out. It's amazing what someone can do once fear has been conquered. Annie stood there, poked her nose through the gate, and actually touched Sinbad's nose. Either he was so shocked that she touched him, or he was so frightened of her, because he didn't hang around for anything else to happen. He ran off as fast as he could and joined his wives; there's safety in numbers.

Annie stood and watched him go, feeling very proud of herself that she'd made the effort to say hello, and she didn't feel frightened at all; in fact, she felt marvellous. At last she was her own person and could go anywhere she liked, because she no longer needed someone to hold her hoof or walk by her side. Now she was as brave as she wanted to be.

When the Moon Turned Orange

Once upon another day down on the farm, there was lots of noise coming from all quarters. The horses and ponies were kicking up quite a fuss and neighing to each other. The dogs were barking, the chickens were clucking, the pigs were oinking and grunting as they ran round and round in circles, and the sheep were baa baaing. Everyone had gone crazy. Bo decided he had to go and find out what all the fuss was about. He'd never heard so many animals all trying to speak and move around at the same time. Who was going to tell him what was going on and more importantly, who would tell him the truth? Bo decided Monty would know, as he went everywhere except that he couldn't quite squeeze into the tiny spaces that cats can find themselves in, nor could he listen from the rooftops. But obviously, while he'd been asleep inside the nice, warm, and cosy house, something had happened through the night that had resulted in so much noise and concern to everyone down on the farm.

"Monty," he shouted, in order to be heard. "Over here by the feed room." Bo saw him look around to see who had called his name, but he couldn't quite work out where it came from. Thinking as fast as he could, Bo dashed up the telegraph pole and jumped down onto the roof of the feed room. "Monty, over here," he shouted again, hoping this time he'd see him. Bo watched as Monty flicked his ears back and forth, as he tried to find out where his name had been called from, so he shouted again. "Monty, look up," and hey presto he saw him. "I need to talk to you, urgently. Meet me by the feed room," he shouted as he watched Monty make his way toward the fence that separated the main yard from the little yard where the feed room was. Bo then made his way back down the telegraph pole as Monty climbed through the fence, which was his favourite party trick, because he was the only one of all the little ponies that could do it.

Away from all the noise and movement of everyone else, they were able to hear themselves talk.

"Hi Bo, what's so urgent that you need to talk to me?" Monty asked, as his back legs followed his body through the fence. "Any food about, now I'm here? Some tasty titbit or two would be very nice."

"No, there's no food, so don't bother looking. I need to know what's going on. Why is everyone so upset? Has something happened? What did I miss?" Bo asked in a hurry.

"Hang on a minute, settle yourself down, Bo, and then I'll tell you what I know." Monty spoke in such a grown-up, matter-of-fact way. He quite liked this new rank Bo had promoted him to, where he was being asked questions. He felt quite important. "The moon turned orange and fell out of the sky."

"That's serious, isn't it?" Bo asked with a frown etched upon his little face. He was sure that the moon shouldn't fall out of the sky. Some nights when he was out hunting, he'd look up and see the big, silvery moon shining up there surrounded by hundreds of twinkling stars. He knew, too, that some nights there was no moon to see, and it would be extra dark. These were really good nights for hunting. But to fall out of the sky, that didn't sound right at all. Being concerned and worried, he wanted to know more. "Tell me what you know, Monty; this is serious."

"Well, apparently Eddie, the owl, saw it all. He said he'd never seen the moon so big, so close, and so orange," Monty said with such calmness.

"Orange?" Bo questioned. He'd never seen an orange moon before. "Sorry Monty, please carry on. I want to know everything."

"I'll carry on, but no more interruptions, okay!" Monty said as he looked down at his little friend and saw the worried look on his tiny face. "Well, Eddie thought that as the moon was that close, if he could fly fast enough, he'd be able to land on it, and then he'd be famous and be known throughout the land as 'Eddie the first owl on the moon.' But as much as he tried to fly as fast as he could, flapping his wings as hard and as fast as they'd go, he couldn't reach the moon before it disappeared."

"He saw it disappear," Bo said in a voice that trembled with the shocking news he'd just heard. Now his tiny face wore a startled look as well as a frown.

"Shall I continue?" Monty asked, getting a little irate with his friend. He was just getting into the flow of his story.

"Sorry," Bo said, making himself even smaller, as he didn't want to upset his friend anymore than he already had. "I promise I'll keep quiet until you finish your story."

"This is no story," Monty said in a matter-of-fact voice. "I'm telling it to you as it was told to me by my mum. Apparently, according to Eddie, who told it to everyone he could, he actually saw the moon fall out of the sky. One minute it was there and then it was gone."

Bo just couldn't help himself, he had to know. "What happened next?"

Monty just looked at him and carried on. "A lot of ruffled and flying feathers," he laughed; he couldn't help himself. "Eddie was so busy watching the moon fall from the sky, he forgot to look where he was going and hit a tree. So instead of seeing the moon, he started seeing stars."

"Ouch," Bo winced at the thought of it. "I bet that hurt."

"More his pride than anything else," Monty laughed. "He had to pick himself up, smooth his feathers down, and fly off again as quickly as he could, because he needed to spread the news that the moon had turned orange and had fallen out of the sky, and we all needed to take care and be very watchful."

"Watchful over what?" Bo asked, with a puzzled looked on his little face.

"What will happen to us?" Monty asked Bo, hoping that maybe he might be able to answer this question, as no one else seemed to be able to, which was why everyone was upset.

"Nothing," Bo replied, in a grown-up, matter-of-fact way. "Everyone has to remain cool and calm, because trust me, the moon will be back tonight."

"How do you know this?" Monty asked, looking at the tiny cat sitting very close to him with a new level of respect, thinking to himself, *How does such a tiny animal know so much?*

"I just know, trust me, you'll see," Bo replied, feeling quite pleased and smug that he knew the answer to what had appeared to be such a big problem for everyone else on the farm. He wondered, though why Eddie had become so worried. Perhaps it was the bump on his head.

"Yes, but what if it doesn't come back tonight?" Monty asked, still not convinced that Bo knew all of the answer.

"If it doesn't come back, we carry on as normal; but, it will be back." Bo gave his friend a reassuring pat on his hoof. "Trust me, everything will be fine."

"How do you know so much, Bo?" Monty asked his friend, looking for as much comfort as he could from this tiny cat.

"I watch, I observe, I look, and I listen."

"Aren't they all the same?" Monty asked. It was his turn to wear the frown this time. He wanted to scratch his head, but he couldn't, as he didn't want to disturb Bo, who was sitting very close to his hoof.

"No, they're not," Bo replied, feeling really good about how he felt. Monty had made him feel really big and important by trusting him and asking his advice. He felt much bigger than the tiny cat he really was. "You see Monty, we can all see without seeing, and listen without hearing, because we can all pick and choose what we want to see and hear. Like the way you choose the type of grass you eat. Do you look at the colour of it, or the shape of it, and which bits do you ignore because you don't like the taste of them? How do you choose, because to me, all grass looks the same. But you know differently, because you have to know."

"Do I?" Monty replied, although he wasn't sure what Bo was really trying to say. "I'm a little confused, Bo. I thought I saw and heard everything, and what's eating got to do with it? I never even think about looking at the grass because I just know what will taste nice and what won't."

"See, I was right," Bo said as he cleaned his whiskers. "There are some things you don't need to take any notice of, as they're not important to you. You don't even look at the grass you eat because you automatically know where to look for the tasty stuff. I bet you don't even take any notice of a bird flying out of the hedgerow, or a rabbit running across the field, because you know they won't hurt you, and you don't need to chase after them for food, either. Do you know that there are some nights when the moon never shines, and we're all still here?"

"I didn't know that," Monty replied, feeling a little upset with himself that he'd never even noticed that the moon didn't always shine.

"It's okay," Bo reassured him. "You don't need to know because when the moon comes out, you're normally fast asleep on your cosy bed of straw. I know about the moon, because I do my hunting at night, when it's dark. Some nights when the moon is so full and bright and I can see his big, round face smiling down on us, that it's too bright to hunt, because just as I can see the rabbits and the mice, they can see me, and they run away. So you see, Monty, it isn't important for you to know about the cycles of the moon, but it is for me."

"Have you ever spoken to the man-in-the-moon and if so, what did he say to you?" Monty asked Bo, feeling sure that he must have done, because he knew so much about it. He was very impressed by what Bo had told him so far and felt so much better already, now that he knew the moon hadn't really fallen out of the sky.

"I spoke to him only yesterday," Bo replied, puffing his chest out to make himself look a little bigger. "I was out hunting and he told me to tell everyone not to worry if he went away, because he'll always come back, as he goes away quite often. In fact, we could set our watches and our calendars by his comings and goings, if we had any, because he is always on time. He also said that if we look up into the night sky and see him shining down on us, he'll look different each night, because he's always changing. Every night he changes his position in the sky and how much we see of him changes, too. Some nights we don't see him because he's invisible, then he comes back, and then we have to keep looking each night to see him growing bigger and bigger, until we see his full face smiling down on us. Then for a short time, we see him getting smaller and smaller and then he disappears again until he's ready to come back, and so the cycle of the moon continues. He also said that because we're constantly seeing him change, we shouldn't be afraid of any changes in our lives, as they're happening around us all of the time. So we all need to have more fun, stop worrying, and enjoy ourselves, because worry is like a cat's tail, it moves all by itself."

"Did he really say all of that?" Monty asked, feeling very proud that he had a friend called Bo, who had spoken to the man-in-the-moon.

"No," Bo laughed, "I made the last bit up to make you smile."

"Oh Bo, you're such a very special and magical cat." Monty laughed with his friend. He really did feel much better now. "I better go and tell the others what you've told me, so that they can smile, too."

"Next time the moon turns orange and falls out of the sky, I'll show you how I walk through walls and that's a promise," Bo laughed as he waved good-bye to his friend. "Don't forget to tell them everything."

"I won't," Monty called after him. He was sure he could make everyone understand that the moon would be back tonight and that it was normal for it to disappear, it was just doing what it always did, so there was nothing to be afraid of, it would be back. He wasn't sure though, if he could convince them that Bo could walk through walls. Well, there was definitely one way of finding out, the only problem was, they were going to have to wait until the moon turned orange and fell out of the sky.

Sleepy Time

Well, howdy partner, shall we have a stroll around the farm this morning and see what everyone is doing? You may think that all the animals do is eat and sleep; that's nearly true, but they do other things, too. Like humans, they need to rest after they've eaten as it helps the stomach digest the food. They could go running around the field, but it might just be a little uncomfortable. Perhaps you've tried it? Oh, you have, and did your tummy feel a bit funny? Did it make funny sounds? It did? Well, it does that without running around, so that's okay then; but, it's much better to let your meal go down before you start running around. The horses and ponies like to have little naps during the day; it helps the grass that they've eaten go all the way down into their tummies.

On a nice sunny morning, you'll often catch the horses and ponies having a little nap, while they enjoy the warmth of the sun on their backs. They usually do this standing up, but occasionally, they may lie down for their mid-morning rest time. Do you like to take little naps? Do you have rest times when you're quiet, or are you on the go all day long?

Just imagine for a moment. I'd better make sure that you have a good imagination first. Can you make pictures in your head? Did I see you nodding your head? I did, well, that must mean that you're very good at making pictures in your head. I'm so pleased, because that means that you can help me.

So, let's imagine that you're walking around the farm with

me and we're going to count how many big horses there are enjoying this morning's sunshine. So, can you make a picture in your head of five big horses? I'm sure you know what a horse looks like. They have four legs, a long tail, a long neck with a long mane, and a big head at the end of the neck. See, I knew you'd be good at this.

Now, there are five big horses that live together in a herd. Two of these horses, Annie and Misty Blue, like to be together and sometimes Big Jed joins them, like he's done today. Now, do you think they're asleep or awake? You're so good at this, you got it right, they're asleep all lined up in a row, all three of them. Their eyes are closed and their heads are held down low, showing that they're relaxed, that is, they're not on alert, waiting for something to happen. Do you know how to rest and relax? You do, that's so good. Do you rest with your eyes closed, and do you go to sleep very quickly? You do, that's really, really good. I've heard that some children find it very hard to go to sleep. It would be very good, wouldn't it, if the horses could tell them what to do, especially as they don't have a problem closing their eyes and nodding off. Do you think we should ask them? I saw you shake your head then. You're absolutely right, we shouldn't disturb their sleep. We wouldn't like it, would we, if we were suddenly woken up without warning? Let's just watch them for a while so that we can enjoy the warmth, too.

Can you imagine how cosy they must be feeling, with that warm sunshine on their backs? Do you think it's like snuggling down under your bedclothes and feeling all warm and cosy in your bed?

As they're standing there, the warmth of the sun begins to soothe them, and everything is so calm, quiet, and peaceful, their tummies are full, and there is no work to do. Everything can switch off. No television to watch, no music to listen to, no computers to play with, no telephones ringing, only peace, calm, and quiet. Their ears are still working, though; they keep moving them, just to make sure that nothing is happening around them, they wouldn't want to miss out on anything. No – it's all quiet, everything is quiet and calm, and so their eyes begin to get a little heavier, and their lids begin to close once more. At first they open and close their eyes several times as they try to fight this feeling of being so calm, so peaceful, and so quiet, but the effort of trying to stay awake is just too much and they have to give in, so they close their eyes, shutting them tightly. Can you close your eyes now like the horses? Good, and because they're shut, it means that everything else is shut out, too, so that nothing can disturb you now. No sudden sounds or people moving around can disturb that sleep.

You've gone to sleep now and will wake up when your body tells you to. You won't move, because you don't need to move. You can now remain asleep and enjoy the warmth and cosiness that comes with the peace and quiet of sleep time.

Don't worry if you need to get up in the night, that's okay, because a visit to the bathroom shows that you're in control and can wake up whenever you want to. However, there's another part of you that stays asleep, because it knows how important a good night's rest is to your body and to your mind, so that when you get back into your bed, your eyes will close just as soon as your head touches the pillow and you'll feel all cosy and warm again, which means that you'll go right back into that deep sleep, so easily that you don't even have to think about it. Just like the horses enjoying their rest time in the warmth, knowing that nothing can disturb that pleasant feeling of sleep. And in the morning when it's time to get up, you'll be wide awake and ready for the new day ahead. You'll be ready to enjoy it in every way, because your body will feel so calm and good. Your mind will feel happy, calm, and alert and you'll feel much better about yourself, too. You'll feel more confident and happier because you enjoyed a restful and peaceful night's sleep.

If you loved this book, would you please provide a review at Amazon.com?

9 781628 570557